Lost Heritage

Royals in slave clothes

Table of Contents

A 19th-Century African tale of uncommon slavery

Written
By
Phyllis Asibor

Disclaimer

"LOST HERITAGE: ROYALS in slave clothes" is a work of fiction. It is an inaccurate historical depiction of 19th-century African royalty and slave trade practice.

Any similarities between living or dead people, current or past works of art, actual events, names, places, characters, and incidents are completely coincidental.

This book contains some sensitive material, reader discretion and parental guidance is advised.

Copyright

Dedication

THIS FIRST BOOK AND all my future books are dedicated to the one true God. He is God Almighty, the father of our Lord, Jesus Christ. All the glory regarding this book and all the glory regarding my life belongs to Him.

Acknowledgment

TO ALL THE PEOPLE WHO saw potential in me, and urged me to actualize it. Thank you.

I hereby acknowledge my entire writing team, all my family, and friends that supported and assisted me during the creation of this book. Thank you.

Special thanks to Dasilver and Latoya who had to listen to me talk about my book incessantly.

Thank you.

Richard Asibor Memorial

I ACKNOWLEDGE MY LATE father, Richard Asibor. He was a renowned Editor at the Nigerian Television Authority and the Chief Cinematographer and owner of Video One Productions, Benin City, Nigeria.

He gave me my first fiction novel to read while I was in the fifth grade. The book was titled "My Father's Car." I read that book multiple times before I finally passed his grueling tests of reading comprehension.

His corrections to my written work thereafter were endless. He flawlessly edited my writing numerous times. He demanded excellence and refused to settle for less. He succeeded in planting a love for fiction in my heart. Today, as my first editor, I salute and acknowledge my late father's efforts.

With much ado, I give you my debut novel; " Lost Heritage: Royals in slave clothes."

About The Book

AGE-OLD AFRICAN CUSTOMS, ancient traditions, the slave trade, and unusual circumstances have enticed and entrapped Oba Ookpala; the King of 19th-century West African Benoni-Obadom, to live life without his faith in God, his beloved Queen Iredia, and their children.

There is a renowned Portuguese pirate on the prowl. His specialty is slave cargo. Royals were sold as slaves. Different *types of slavery* abounded in the land.

There is a missing pregnant Queen. She possibly carries the heir to the throne of Benoni Obadom.

Will the love of the royal couple triumph over the trials of unusual slavery? Will the slave trade give back what it has snatched from this royal African family?

With the *intervention of the Christian God,* will the lost Queen and the heir of Benoni be recovered?

Join me on this voyage, as these questions and more are answered within the enthralling pages of *"Lost Heritage: Royals in slave clothes."*

Chapter 1: A Silent Funeral

IN THE MID EIGHTEEN hundreds, Old Oba Eluu of the Benoni Obadom passed away from old age after four decades of ruling Benoni. It was time for Benoni to commence its funeral rites and traditions following the demise of its Oba. The queens of the Oba were going to be buried alive along with the body of the Oba, accompanied by their seven slaves.

Efe, the favorite aide of Prince Ookpala, the third son of the deceased Oba, walked into the chamber of the Prince. He had confined himself in one of the rooms of the Red Palace. He was mourning for his deceased father and soon-to-be deceased mother.

"Prince Ookpala?" Efe asked as he stepped inside the chamber.

The prince stared out his window and his eyes were fixed on a particular sight - his mother was being escorted to the Priest Ground. Efe ran to the window and drew the curtain to spare Ookpala the torment of watching his mother walk to her death.

"You don't deserve to see this," Efe told Ookpala as he reached out his hand to draw the curtain away, trying to catch a last glimpse of the queen.

"I have failed her. I'm helpless here while my mother marches silently to be killed by those old snobs!" Ookpala sobbed.

Efe glanced at his feet. He didn't have anything left to say to a man who had just seen his mother healthy and alive for the last time.

OBA ELUU'S THREE WIVES were escorted to the Priest Ground which was occupied by the Red Palace's priests. They were seated on three chairs beneath the platform of the Priest Ground.

As the widows remained seated, three priests approached them with white sheets and scarlet coral-beaded necklaces. The widows kept their sight fixed at their feet as the priests covered them with white sheets across their chests along with the red coral-beaded necklaces.

The row behind the widows was occupied by the seven slaves who were standing behind them, awaiting their grave fate. They remained silent as they watched the queens get dressed for their eternal journey.

A balding man, dressed in white robes ascended the platform and stood upright. It was Chief Ajala, the chief priest of the Priest Ground of the Benoni kingdom.

"We have gathered here to witness the final rites of Oba Eluu and his entourage to the afterlife. The entourage is comprised of his three beloved wives and seven slaves. Oba Eluu has ascended to a world from which he won't return, but he won't be alone in his afterlife. His queens will embark on the journey and accompany him for eternity, " Priest Ajala said. "Priests! Prepare the slaves for their final journey."

He gestured to the priests standing alongside the widows.

The priests painted the slaves' faces with liquid chalk, gave them white masks, and took off their tunics, leaving them bare-chested. All of them were given the same white sheets, which were tied across their waists as they prepped for their own funerals.

"My Queens, please honor your great Oba by drinking the water that was used to wash his corpse. It will lead you to your Oba so you can join him in his afterlife," Priest Ajala said to the widows as they were approached by priests holding small calabashes of water.

From the date of their royal marriages, the widows had already been groomed to accept this grim fate. It was the tradition of Benoni that the queens would accompany their Oba to the afterlife. They had no choice and voiced no objections. The widows drank the water which contained poison.

They got up from their chairs and then, without another word, they walked to their wooden coffins and lay down in eternal rest.

The chief priest addressed the slaves.

"All of you have served the Oba until he has breathed his last. Your life has been that of service, and you are bound to your Oba. You will remain together in the afterlife as well. Accept these last tokens as Benoni's gratitude for your service and loyalty to your Oba. It will mark the beginning of your eternal journey," the chief priest continued.

The slaves were given emerald stones set in bronze rings which symbolized that they were *"separated for royal sacrifice in Benoni."* They wore the rings, and the priests gestured to them to kiss the rings. Once their lips came in contact with the emerald stone, they turned a purplish color which quickly spread; it was the kiss of death as the rings were poisonous.

"Your final journey awaits you," Priest Ajala announced. The slaves walked to their coffins and were laid down for their eternal journey to the afterlife.

After a few minutes, a priest stepped up and put his finger beneath the nostrils of the widows and slaves, checking on them, one after another.

"They have departed," he said to Ajala.

Once the priests had confirmed that the widows and slaves were no longer alive, servants of the Red Palace lifted the coffins onto their shoulders, moving them from the Priest's Ground to their final resting place.

The procession of coffins came into the graveyard silently, as Oba Eluu's three sons, family members, and members of the council waited at the graveyard of the Priest's Ground. The sons appeared uptight, not allowed to shed a single tear as the coffins of their parents were laid out in front of them. Prince Ookpala's eyes began to get damp as he saw the coffin of his mother in front of him, but Efe elbowed him softly.

"The Oba's descendants are not supposed to shed tears during the funeral. You can't be weak," Efe whispered to nineteen-year-old Ookpala.

As the coffin of Oba Eluu was lowered into his grave, Priest Ajala gestured at Prince Nosa to come forward. Prince Nosa was the oldest son of the departed Oba and his rightful heir.

Prince Nosa grabbed a hand full of red-colored sand and threw it on the coffin of his father and mother while maintaining a stern posture, not letting anyone witness his emotions. After he had partaken in the funeral tradition, Osu, Oba Eluu's second son, walked forward and threw sand over the coffins of his parents as well.

The last one to come forward to throw the red sand was Prince Ookpala, Oba Eluu's youngest son. He threw the sand at his parents' coffin, with tears streaming down his cheeks with a huge sigh of defiance. He did not care about the tradition of not showing emotion during the burial of the royal party.

Efe, Prince Ookpala's personal aide, squeezed his hand, whispering in his ear, "Stop weeping, my prince. Any show of emotion during the burial of the Oba is forbidden."

Ookpala just shook his head without any response.

Chief Maina, the Head of the Palace Chiefs, put his hand on Crown Prince Nosa's shoulder, patting it gently as he watched his parents get buried.

"These are challenging times, but you must understand your role in the kingdom. Your father wanted you to ascend the throne swiftly after he left this world. You and your queen are responsible for Benoni's fate now," Maina said as he looked at Nosa and his wife, Princess Aboma who was standing beside him.

"I know my responsibility. You don't have to hammer it in me," Prince Nosa responded curtly.

Princess Aboma immediately excused herself and with her handmaiden, Osaze. No one paid them any attention as they hurried out of the graveyard.

"CLOSE THE DOORS," PRINCESS Aboma commanded Osaze as soon as she entered her chamber. Osaze closed the door, ensuring no one was lurking around to eavesdrop on their conversation.

"He must meet his father in the afterlife BEFORE he ascends the throne," Aboma said in a serious voice. If it does not happen in that order, he will already be the Oba, and both of us will be buried alive with him!

"Why don't you lie down for a while?" Osaze suggested as she pulled a pillow for Aboma.

"It's not the time for rest. We have to hurry with this matter. What about the palm wine?" Aboma asked as she paced around the chamber.

"I'm working on it," Osaze answered.

"It should have been ready by now. We have to prepare it before his coronation seclusion," Aboma emphasized.

Osaze and Aboma's conversation was interrupted by a loud thud outside the doors of their chamber. Osaze ran to see the cause of the intrusion but when she opened the door, she found her younger sister, Mishkia standing outside.

"Who is there?" Aboma screamed.

"Just a maid," Osaze responded. "I will return shortly."

Osaze grabbed the hand of her sister, Mishkia, and dragged her across the hallway.

"What were you doing there?" Osaze whispered to her sister.

"Are you planning to kill the prince?" Mishkia whispered.

"Did you hear everything?" Osaze asked, stunned.

"Yes," Mishkia answered. "My sister Osaze is conspiring against the crown." Princess Aboma wants to kill the prince so she does not die as his queen.

"It's not that simple. You need to understand the reason," Osaze said.

"Understand what?" Mishkia asked.

"Prince Nosa is why Princess Aboma lost her twins," Osaze explained.

"Twins?" Mishkia asked.

"Yes. You know of the evil forest, right? Do you know why it is called that?" Osaze asked.

"Of course! Everyone does. It's because it has ghosts and such." Mishkia awaited her elder sister's response.

"Benoni wants us to believe it's a forest haunted by spirits and ghosts, but that is not true. They are the ones that put the ghosts there. It's the place where all the twins that are born in Benoni are buried. It's also the place where Aboma's twins were killed!"

"I know our people kill twins. I hate that custom" Mishkia leaned against the window sill as she crossed her ankles.

"There is no place for twins in Benoni. They are considered a bad omen, so you never hear about them. They're killed before they are even given a chance to grow up."

"Why is Prince Nosa being blamed for this?" Mishkia asked.

"Prince Nosa was the leader of the band that snatched away Aboma's twin daughters when she was a commoner from her. She had been married for only ten months. She was also widowed after her previous husband hung himself on the same day his twins were killed," Osaze explained.

Mishkia's eyes widened. She covered her mouth with her palm as she listened to Princess Aboma's history.

"Not only did Nosa kill Aboma's twins in the evil forest, but he also forced her to marry him since his last two wives passed away during childbirth without any heirs," Osaze continued. "He longed for a fertile woman and when he saw

Aboma, a commoner birthed effortlessly with twins, he became hellbent on marrying her and he succeeded.

Her marriage to him was barely two months after her husband's death! Notwithstanding, Prince Nosa has been a cruel husband to her. Mishkia, you do not need me to detail his cruelties to you. Again, you are well aware of them."

"Ahhh. I am already aware that Princess Aboma has indeed suffered before becoming our princess and continues to suffer as the wife of our Prince," Mishkia empathized with anguish in her voice.

Osaze nodded her head in agreement.

"But that does not justify plotting against the crown," she added viciously.

"I arrived in the Red Palace with Aboma as her hand-maiden. She gave birth to Uyi after a year, but Aboma swore to subject Prince Nosa to the same fate as her children and late husband," Osaze explained. "I remember her words vividly. She told me that the heir Nosa desperately yearns for would be the one to usurp his throne. She promised to ensure that Nosa joins her deceased husband. She plans to join her deceased family in the afterlife when she gets buried with Nosa."

"Interesting, I am no talebearer, but I am not in support of this plot. Uyi, Princess Aboma's son, is just eleven years old. How will he usurp the throne? Both of you are bound to get in big trouble for this. My ears are closed. Please do not involve me in treason," Mishkia said as she lifted her palms up.

"You ask too many questions. Who is going to involve you? Please leave quickly before the princess finds you here," Osaze responded.

PRINCESS ABOMA BEGAN looking for Osaze, who had left her chamber a while ago. She searched through the hallways before finding her heading into the maids' chambers.

"Osaze," she called out.

"I need to take care of the palm wine," Osaze said.

"Come here," Aboma instructed.

When Osaze was nearer, she gave her more instructions in a low voice.

"As soon as the funeral is over, the priests will head out of the graveyard to the Priest Ground to prepare for the coronation ceremony of Crown Prince Nosa," Aboma stated. "For Nosa to be crowned the Oba of Benoni, remember that tradition demands that he goes through a period of seclusion which would last for seven days, followed by his coronation. No one is aware of the rituals done during the ceremony as it is kept hidden from people. It has to be done before the coronation ceremony when he can't get out of the Priest Ground."

"I understand," Osaze nodded before leaving.

"WE ARE LEAVING BENONI," Prince Ookpala, the third prince of the kingdom, said to his wife, Iredia after the funeral.

"What are you talking about?" Iredia asked.

Ookpala guided Iredia to the corner of the hallway.

"These barbaric traditions of burying the Oba's widows and slaves with the deceased Oba don't serve anyone. My perfectly healthy mother had to die because her husband died. Thanks to a horrible ancient tradition! She didn't deserve that. No one deserves it," he declared. "I can't stand to watch the barbaric customs of Benoni anymore. I refuse to be a part of it. We have to leave. We will not be coming back."

"Where will we go? I'm with child. I am practically due for delivery any day now. We have to be careful. What if I deliver on the road? I am afraid," Iredia massaged her heavily pregnant stomach with her right palm, while her left palm massaged her lower back.

"I will look after you," Ookpala reassured her.

"You will be my midwife?" she responded incredulously.

"Yes, I will!" he stated firmly. "Just trust me."

"My prince, the midwifery lessons you have been taking from the village maternity must have you feeling very confident. However, I insist we go with a midwife from the village. I will not put my life and that of our child in the hands of your training," Iredia waddled out of the room, leaving Prince Ookpala to resolve the problem.

SOON, OOKPALA WENT to the Great Hall, where the council was sitting to decide the fate of Benoni after Oba Eluu's funeral.

"And about the seclusion-"

Crown Prince Nosa stopped abruptly while conversing with the council as he saw his younger brother Ookpala walk in.

"I am leaving bloody Benoni with my wife, Iredia," Prince Ookpala told his brother Nosa.

Prince Nosa got up from his seat and tried to persuade Ookpala not to leave. He reached for Ookpala's shoulder, but Ookpala shrugged his hand away.

"What my mother suffered today is nothing short of abominable. My wife won't be subjected to the same torment that my mother had to suffer today," he stated firmly. "Also, my wife is pregnant. For all I know, she may have twins. I can't imagine my children being killed when she delivers if they are twins. I can't take that chance. It may be okay with you that your wife will be buried alive when you cease to be. It is not okay with me."

"These are our traditions..." Prince Nosa began to say.

"I don't want anything to do with my lineage. I don't want anyone to come looking for me. I am no longer from Benoni. None of my children are!" Ookpala declared.

"You can't leave the Obadom, and you cannot deny your heritage. It is in your blood," Nosa reasoned with Ookpala. "We have had this conversation before. Traditions and customs are exactly what they are. We have no choice in the matter."

"As a prince, I may not have a choice. But, you, as the Oba have a choice," Prince Ookpala pointed out.

"It's not that...." Nosa began, but Ookpala cut him off.

I am done having these arguments. My mother is dead already. You'll have to kill me to stop me from leaving; I am done with Benoni. Consider me dead. I just came to say goodbye and confirm I still have your consent to leave with the palace midwife?" Ookpala started walking towards the exit of the Great Hall.

" You can take the midwife with you, but remember to swap her out with Princess Iredia's personal maid. She can have either the personal maid or the midwife, not both, Nosa responded as he sat down to continue his meeting.

"I will do so," Ookpala nodded his head and walked out the door.

EFE, OOKPALA'S TRUSTED aide, Ookpala, and Iredia went ahead with their plan to leave the kingdom, refusing to listen to Crown Prince Nosa, the second Prince Osu, or the council of chiefs' entreaties.

Ookpala got on his horse while Efe rode another that pulled the carriage in which palace midwife Oghale and Princess Iredia were sitting as they departed from Benoni.

Chapter 2: Revenge

IT WAS PAST MIDNIGHT and Princess Aboma couldn't find a moment of peace. She kept pacing restlessly in circles in her chamber, waiting for an update on events from her loyal Osaze. She glanced outside her window, which overlooked the courtyard every now and then, and then looked at the door that Osaze could knock on at any given moment.

"Princess," Osaze's voice echoed in the hallway.

Princess Aboma ran to the door to let Osaze in.

"I told you to knock," Aboma whispered as soon as Osaze entered.

"I have been kept up all night by the servants in the kitchen. I'm starting to lose my senses now, but I have good news. It's ready," Osaze's lips curved into a subtle grin as she informed Aboma.

"And are we certain about our man?" Aboma inquired.

"He has been serving in the Priest Ground for five years now. He doesn't have any loyalty to the priests. He's on our side," Osaze reassured a restless Aboma.

Aboma listened to Osaze as she looked outside the window. Finally, she saw the sight she had been waiting for the entire night. The one who had massacred her twins brutally was being taken to the Priest Ground, where he was going to observe a seclusion period that would last for seven days.

"Is he going to be able to inform us about the events that will take place on the Coronation Ground?" Aboma asked as her eyes remained fixed on the departure of her husband, Prince Nosa.

"I'm afraid it will remain a mystery for us. The priests and servants are sworn to secrecy regarding the rituals followed in the coronation section of the Priest Ground," Osaze said.

The chilly wind blew through the window, making Aboma shiver.

"I just felt a strange chill. As if someone walked over my grave," Aboma mused quietly. Then, shaking herself, she said, "Never mind."

Soon, the wind started roaring and turned into a rainstorm. Osaze rushed to shut the windows, but Aboma stopped her.

"I need to see him go. I wish to see him die," Aboma murmured as her gaze rested on the silhouette of Prince Nosa, who was accompanied by Maina and the palace guards.

Osaze reached across from behind Aboma. She pulled the bamboo windows shut, stating, "No need to watch him enter the Priest Ground anymore. Your orders will be followed to the letter, my princess."

JUST BEFORE PRINCE Nosa could walk through the gates of the Priest Ground, Maina grabbed his hand from behind, making him stand still.

"You won't be entering alone," Maina told Prince Nosa.

Prince Nosa heard the sound of footsteps approaching him and turned around to find out that his son, Uyi was there too.

"Good, I was expecting you to accompany me, the same way I accompanied my deceased father years ago," Nosa stretched his palm out to his thirteen-year-old heir.

"Immediately after you transition from prince to Oba; the heir will be the first server to the Oba of Benoni. It's a custom that is followed by the incoming Oba of Benoni, my prince. You did the same for your father, now Uyi will serve you during your recovery," Maina nodded his head.

Together, Prince Nosa and his son Uyi entered the Priest Ground and made their way to the holy place of the Coronation Ground - a sacred section of the Priest Ground. The ceremony started shortly after the arrival of Benoni's prince and the rightful heir to the throne.

PRINCE OOKPALA'S PARTY had been traveling east for several days the bumping of the carriage was uncomfortable for Princess Iredia. She had been mostly sleeping, when she was jolted awake as the horse-drawn carriage stopped.

"We will stop here for a while," Ookpala said. "Let us rest, eat and get the horses something to eat as well."

Efe complied and went into the bushes in search of some firewood.

"My love, are you okay? We will make camp here for the night," Ookpala informed his wife as he dismounted from his horse.

"Where exactly are we going?" Iredia fussed. "I don't find it funny. I wish you were the pregnant one."

Ookpala burst out laughing.

"Thank the heavens, I am not pregnant, my darling Iredia," Ookpala stated. "If I were pregnant, that would not be funny."

"Of course not. That's why it's okay for you to randomly decide to leave Benoni when you know my condition," Iredia scolded him.

"Iredia, let us be serious now. What if you give birth to twins? You were the one who told me that you dreamt that you gave birth to twins. You are very much aware of what happens to twins at birth in Benoni. We don't want to lose our children if this pregnancy results in twins, do we?" Ookpala reasoned.

"No, but it's just a dream. What if, after all this hassle, I give birth to a single child? Did it occur to you that I might go into labor on the road?" Iredia fanned with a dried palm frond hand-held fan. "I am nervous. Childbearing is difficult on its own without the added certainty of sufficient help when in labor."

"Don't worry, my wife. I took my maternity lessons seriously. Also, we have Oghale with us. She is very experienced. If I have to deliver your baby, I promise not to faint," Ookpala reassured her.

"Hmphhh," Iredia stuck her tongue out at her nineteen-year-old husband.

Shortly after, Efe walked back into the camp with some hay for the horses and firewood for the campfire so they could cook their food. Oghale helped in roasting some yams for dinner.

WHEN THE SUN DAWNED, and the sunlight lit the Coronation Ground, the stains of blood on the ground and the stains of blood on the idols of Otun, the god of Benoni, became visible. Prince Nosa was lying on the raised platform with blood spilling out of his chest from seven cuts, but he was breathing.

"Chief Maina, fetch Prince Uyi, Prince Nosa is no more. He is now Oba Nosa of Benoni Kingdom. He has passed his test." Head Priest Ajala gestured for Prince Nosa's son who was dressed in a white loin clothe, and secluded away from the happenings of the Coronation Ground within the Priest Ground.

Chief Maina fetched Prince Uyi, and handed him the palm wine in a calabash that was meant to be consumed by the new Oba of Benoni.

"Make your father drink it," Head Priest Ajala told Uyi.

Uyi took the calabash from the hands of Chief Maina and he inched closer and hovered the calabash near Oba Nosa who was barely conscious. He tried to convince his father to drink but he kept shaking his head.

"My Oba, you must drink from the calabash to complete the ceremony. Your heir must be your first server," Chief Maina insisted.

"Father, look here," Uyi said, as he drank from the calabash. "You just need to take a sip."

After much persuasion, Oba Nosa agreed to drink from the calabash. As Oba Nosa was drinking from the cup, Prince Uyi started coughing. Soon after he drank from the calabash the new Oba also started doing the same.

Before anyone could understand what was happening, Oba Nosa and Prince Uyi began to puke blood, leaving the priests and chiefs stunned.

Chapter 3: Innocent Blood

PRINCESS ABOMA'S CHAMBER door was blasted open by Osaze, who rushed to her bed to wake her up. She snatched the blanket away from Aboma, forcing her to open her eyes.

"Have you lost your senses?" Aboma yelled.

"He is dead!" Osaze broke the news in a triumphant whisper.

A smile appeared on Aboma's angry face, but it soon disappeared when she noticed that Osaze seemed to be worried. She was shaking all over, and her eyes were red.

"What happened, Osaze?" Aboma asked as she reached for Osaze's cold hands. Osaze looked into her eyes and gathered the courage to tell Aboma the truth.

"Uyi, your only child was there too. He drank the wine as well," she said in a voice that was barely above a whisper.

"You're lying. He couldn't have been. I watched Nosa walk into the Priest Ground with my own two eyes. He was alone. Uyi is fine, isn't he? Tell me you are lying!" Aboma insisted as she shook Osaze.

Osaze shook her head as she stared at the ground, unable to look Aboma in the eye. As Aboma and Osaze both remembered, the handmaiden had pulled the bamboo window shut just before Prince Nosa entered the Priest Ground.

Aboma left Osaze alone in the chamber and ran into the hallway. She was stopped by Prince Osu.

"What is happening?" Aboma screamed at her brother-in-law.

"My Queen, we have lost our new Oba, your husband, and his heir, your son," Prince Osu said.

Aboma fell to the ground, clenching her chest as her screams echoed in the Old Palace. She was helpless. She had lost everything in the blink of an eye. The arrow she aimed at another had pierced through her soul. As queen, she was going to be buried alive with the late Oba! Someone indeed had walked over her grave.

"How?" she howled in pain and sobbed. "How could this happen?"

He had already completed the rites, so he was no longer a prince but Oba.

"The calabash was poisoned. Oba Nosa refused to drink from it, but your son, Uyi, tried to convince his father by drinking from it first. It all happened in a matter of minutes, and they couldn't do anything. Oba Nosa and Prince Uyi both died during the seclusion," Prince Osu tried to comfort a grieving Queen Aboma.

"An Oba for one minute? And now, my fate is death? Princess Aboma sobbed bitterly.

IT WAS ANOTHER DAY of tragedy for Benoni as the people were about to witness the funeral of the rightful heir laid to rest along with his son The people of Benoni were gathered in the courtyard as they awaited the arrival of the priests to declare the tragic news and officiate the funeral rites.

Head Priest Ajala headed the assembly of priests, followed by the coffins of Oba Nosa and Prince Uyi. The coffins were lowered to the ground pending the final procession to their graves. He left the site to officiate the ceremony of Nosa's wife and his slaves' departure for their eternal journey as members of Oba Nosa's eternal procession.

Princess Aboma was seated beneath the raised platform, followed by a queue of seven slaves, including Osaze and others who had served Oba Nosa, Queen Aboma, and Prince Uyi. A goblet containing the poisoned water that was used to wash Oba Nosa's corpse was given to Queen Aboma to drink. She kept sobbing and refusing it.

"My Queen, the water will create a path to your husband. It's necessary that you drink it to commence your final journey," Head Priest Ajala insisted.

"I killed him," Princess Aboma finally said through her tears.

"What are you saying?" Ajala asked.

"I killed your prince and my son. I ordered Osaze to poison the calabash. It was supposed to kill my husband alone, but you allowed my son to drink from it. I didn't know my son would lose his life in my revenge against Nosa! I thought he would die before he became Oba." Princess Aboma wailed.

The ceremony was abruptly cut short by Aboma's declaration.

"What? You are already fated to die today, but we shall not let you pass so peacefully for your crime," Head Priest Ajala said as he took the goblet of poisoned water and threw it to the ground.

He turned to Prince Osu for his judgment. Prince Osu gestured with his finger to take her head.

"Separate her head from her body!" Ajala commanded Esoha, the Head of the Oba's Guard.

Esoha approached the distraught Queen Aboma wielding a giant axe that had a blade that was so sharp it cut through her with one swing. Aboma was beheaded right where she sat, and she bled out on the platform where she was supposed to get poisoned. Osaze, her personal handmaiden, was beheaded alongside the late queen as well.

Mishkia watched with horror and red eyes as she saw the end of the treason planned by the duo.

The bodies were picked up by the palace slaves and sentenced to be thrown into the evil forest without a burial. Nobody was allowed to mourn Queen Aboma's passing. It was declared that her royal status was forever forfeited, and she could only be referred to as Aboma going forward.

The slaves assigned to accompany Prince Nosa and Uyi on their eternal journey were given their poisoned rings to kiss. As they kissed it, they lay down to sleep on their eternal journey.

THE PEOPLE REELED WITH shock at the sudden turn of events, as one tragedy after another followed Benoni. It was declared that Prince Osu, next in line for the throne, would be crowned as the next Oba of Benoni after completing the bloody seclusion ceremony.

Prince Osu knew his responsibility to the throne, and he did what he had to do to secure the future of Benoni. Although he was a sick man with frequent bursts of pain due to his hereditary blood disease, he still went through the process of seclusion and returned as the new Oba of Benoni.

The first order from Oba Osu was the decree that any future Oba's children would no longer be allowed into the Coronation Ground. He also abolished the burial of the Oba's wives, concubines, and slaves with the Oba.

He decreed that rather than burying the Oba's widows and slaves with the departed, ten cows would be slaughtered. The meat for seven of the cows would be distributed among the people of Benoni on the deaths of the future Obas. The meat for the remaining three cows would be shared amongst the priests of the Priest Ground. Henceforth, no human life would be lost following the death of any Oba.

His declaration was met with uproar. The chiefs and priests resisted the new order.

Oba Osu immediately quelled every opposition by executing the Chief Head Priest Ajala! When he asked for any other person not in agreement with his declaration, there was none.

MAINA SAT IN A CHAIR in Esoha's chamber and sipped from a wooden goblet. His eyes were squinted as he stared at a long parchment he held in his hand.

"Benoni is too bloody. What do we gain from death, Esoha?" Maina rubbed his forehead.

"Nothing," Esoha sat on the bed made of red sand, covered with a dry straw mat.

"That is precisely what I aim to change. We can deliver this parchment to the slave trader I told you about. He will take care of the prisoners, while we will get rich," Maina said.

"Are you certain it will work?" Esoha sat down.

"Yes, it will. We have nothing to gain from the executions, and the kingdom has been suffering losses constantly. If the executions are necessary and we are at risk of getting caught, we will leave the prisoners alone," Maina took a sip from his goblet.

"So we are going to sell them to the slave traders? Esoha crossed his arms on his chest.

"Yes," Maina nodded and extended the parchment from his hand to Esoha's as he left the chamber.

THE PEOPLE OF BENONI were worried. Oba Osu refused to get married or have a child. He had watched all his siblings from his mother die very young, one after another as a result of the pain crisis of his hereditary blood disease. He refused to take a wife during his rule. He had no desire to sire heirs.

He declared his half-brother, Prince Ookpala, the rightful heir and the one who was next in line for the throne. He offered a reward for anyone who would give information on his whereabouts.

IT WAS ALMOST TWO MONTHS after the couple, Prince Ookpala and Princess Iredia, left Benoni when Princess Iredia went into labor. They had stopped to get some water from the stream and food supplies in a small town called Yola. While the men were hunting for food and following an antelope they had spied, Princess Iredia's midwife left for the stream for some water. Iredia was left unattended.

Iredia suddenly felt her water break. The pains were strong and gave no notice before their arrival. There was nobody to assist her from her traveling party.

She hunched over and let out a scream as the pain lanced through her pregnant belly.

"Ohh my God, I cannot believe this baby. How can this baby be coming without ooooooh! Help. Help!! Tears ran down her face as sweat poured from her armpits. Her clothes were bloody and wet. Panting, she went down on her knees as she continued to scream for help, cradling her belly on her right forearm, her face contorted with the severity of her contractions.

"What is this? As her hand felt water gush from her vagina, Iredia realized that her baby was not going to wait for the men to return. Fear almost paralyzed her, but in her struggle, she realized, this was life or death.

Her baby was coming now!

As she continued to sob in pain, she reached across her baskets and laid some blankets on the ground between her knees.

"Ohhh my godddd, she sobbed as she reached in between her thighs to feel her vagina, her palm could feel the baby's head pressing against her fingers.

She tried to push, but the baby did not budge. "I might die here she thought to herself. Where is Oghale? Where is Ookpala?

"Somebody, help me!" Kneeling, bent over, her palm cradling her vagina, she screamed. But the carriage was on a bush path. She was unsure if anyone could hear her screams.

She made her way out of the carriage in search of help. As her blood and water seeped through the carriage door, her screams pierced through the quiet evening.

AT ABOUT THAT SAME time, a group of women were walking to the stream. They heard Iredia's scream for help. They sighted Iredia and rushed up to her. She could feel the baby's head literally pushing himself out of her. She adjusted herself to receive her child, and with a mighty push, her son's head exited her vagina into her palm. His body quickly followed, landing in her arm.

Each woman untied one of their two wrappers. Using their wrappers, they created a circle of privacy around her, as her son let out a lusty cry.

One of the women reached down to assist her with the cutting of the cord and yelled.

"They are two! There is another baby! She is having twins!

As there were helping her, Oghale, her midwife, returned from the stream. She quickly joined the women as they birthed the second baby. He was a boy also.

Iredia just had twins. Two boys! They were identical. The women helped her.

Iredia was exhausted after her delivery. Her hair was matted to her forehead, and her tears dried on her face. She told the women she and her party were journeying looking for a new place of settlement.

Placing Iredia's twin sons on her breasts, they gladly offered her and her party a place to stay in Yola, a Christian missionary hostel. The women were Christian missionaries. Iredia and her babies would be welcome and safe.

AS IREDIA THANKED THEM, Prince Ookpala and Efe came back to find Princess Iredia already delivered her twin sons.

" I am so sorry," Prince Ookpala pleaded with his wife on his arrival to find that his Princess Iredia had already delivered their identical twin sons in his absence and she was unattended.

"My Prince, you were not here to witness or assist with the delivery, but I thank you for insisting we leave Benoni, Iredia thanked her husband, as she burst into tears of relief.

"The gods be praised, Ookpala rejoiced, as he danced from place to place; if we had not left Benoni, if we had not left when we did, our children would have been killed soon after their birth.

Efe and the midwife looked at each and nodded as the whole party rejoiced.

"Thank you, Ookpala greeted the missionary women who had assisted Iredia in her delivery.

"We are happy to help, the women responded. I hear you are looking for a place to settle?"

"Yes, we are," Ookpala answered.

"Then please come with us. We are on our way to mass."

"Mass?" what is that, asked Ookpala.

"Mass is the service where we serve our God. His name is Jesus Christ. He is the one that showed up and saved your wife and children during her delivery," one of the missionary women answered him.

"I want to know more of your God, please," Iredia chipped in. "He indeed saved us. My children and I could have died."

The women led Iredia and Ookpala to Christ. They baptized them and the children. They also gave the children the Christian names Peter and Paul.

Oghale decided to follow the women on their missionary journeys. Efe on the other hand, declined to change his religion to Christianity.

Iredia seeing her husband felt safe and passed into a deep sleep.

Chapter 4: Identical Twins

SEVEN YEARS PASSED. Oba Osu's health deteriorated and he rarely ever sat on the throne. His blood disease frequently manifested in pain and cries. Despite his wisdom, the Obadom craved a strong warrior like Oba Eli the Conqueror; but alas, those days were over.

ESOHA, THE CHIEF GUARD, was in the Great Hall along with priests and chiefs.

"He is not going to make it through the night," Esoha told Chief Maina, the Head of the Council of Chiefs.

"Here we are again," responded Chief Maina. "But this time, we don't have any heir left for the Kingdom."

"We have Prince Ookpala," Esoha reminded Maina.

"He is a quitter," Maina said quietly. "He left Benoni a long time ago. He does not deserve to be our Oba."

"He is the rightful heir to the throne," Esoha repeated and Maina sighed with understanding. He knew what the man was trying to say.

"How are we going to find him? He fled Benoni, and no one has any idea where he is," Maina said.

"We can find him if we want to."

"Then we need to do it as soon as possible. Benoni will need a new Oba soon," Maina said, irritated.

IREDIA WAS OUTSIDE in the fields collecting firewood with other women from the village of Yola, where they had settled, when she heard Peter's screams.

At first, she was unsure about what it was, then realized that it was one of her sons, howling and calling for his mother.

She ran out of the field and started looking for him when she realized the voice was coming from the back of a tall tree. Iredia tiptoed to the tree and saw Peter crying on the ground.

"Again?" Iredia raised her eyebrow at Peter.

"I almost reached the second branch, Mama," Peter said, sobbing.

"Then why are you crying?"

"I fell," Peter said as he looked at Iredia with his big innocent eyes.

"That's exactly how I learned climbing. You will fall, and then you will learn eventually. Besides that, you're too small to climb. Why don't you listen to me?" she scolded.

"Paul doesn't fall," Peter said under his breath.

Iredia reached out to Peter. He was still sobbing, but he took her hand and started walking with her. They walked up the hill and stopped at the hut where Ookpala was crafting tools for farming and cultivation.

"My Prince," Iredia called her husband, who was working among several men.

Prince Ookpala saw Iredia outside the hut, standing with their seven-year-old son. He put down the hammer and wiped his sweat before walking to meet her.

"I have asked you to stop calling me that," Prince Ookpala said as he kissed her forehead.

"You'll always be my prince," Iredia replied as she stared into Ookpala's eyes with affection.

Prince Ookpala grinned. Iredia had always been good at expressing her affection. She had been his rock ever since they left Benoni to search for a place they could call home.

Iredia was alone when she gave birth to their first child Peter. However, she never complained about that. Rather, she said it was meant to be like that so they could meet the women who helped her with delivering Paul and also assisted them in settling in Yola.

The journey was difficult, but luckily, Efe, Prince Ookpala's aide, joined them, refusing to leave his prince. Efe had grown up with Prince Ookpala as he was the slave assigned to Ookpala at birth. Efe's presence made their journey less difficult since he was adept at hunting, fishing, and generally surviving outdoors.

Due to Iredia's condition after her delivery, they had to stop in Yola to rest. The villagers were very kind and offered them a place to stay. They never asked them why Prince Ookpala was on the run with his heavily pregnant wife. It was then that Iredia suggested they stay there as it seemed like a safe place to bring up their children.

Prince Ookpala met the head of the village, Chaga, and told him that they had to flee Benoni to save their lives. The head had reservations as he didn't want anyone in his village to be harmed trying to help an outsider. Ookpala promised him that he would never cause any harm to the village.

Chaga eventually agreed to let him and his wife settle in Yola. Despite not knowing his real identity, everyone in the village grew fond of Prince Ookpala. The couple had newborn twin sons when they settled in Yola. The village warmly welcomed the arrival of their children, and they decided to spend the rest of their lives there.

"Peter, why are you crying?" Ookpala asked as he lifted him in his arms. Peter had started sobbing again after seeing his father.

"You need to tell him to stop competing with his brother. He fell again while trying to climb the big tree," Iredia said.

"Little boy, why are you crying? We are going to dance today," Efe said as he came out of the hut. "Now wipe your tears, and let's take you to the festival."

Efe took Peter from Ookpala and put him on his back.

"Are you ready to dance, little prince?" Efe asked.

"Yes," Peter grinned.

Iredia held Ookpala's hand and squeezed it slightly. She felt at home in Yola. She and Ookpala had been having a great time living as commoners. Iredia had never lusted after the crown. All she had wanted was for her and Ookpala to live a peaceful life.

She was very happy with the decision to leave Benoni when she realized that she had birthed twins. Her children were important to her, and if she had been in Benoni when she had them, they would have been thrown into the evil forest shortly after their birth.

Yola was everything Iredia had ever wanted.

"We made the right decision," Iredia said to Ookpala as they walked toward the festivities in the heart of Yola. "I will never question your wisdom again, my love."

"Yes, we did. Perhaps it was our destiny to come here and find a life better than we would have had."

"It's amazing how this place was only going to be a pitstop to another place, yet we ended up here, and look how happy we are," Iredia smiled as she held onto Ookpala's hand.

"My happiness is wherever you and my children are," Ookpala stated as he looked into Iredia's beautiful brown eyes that were beaming in the sunlight.

Ookpala went to Efe's hut to pick up Paul, who was climbing trees when he got there. He was a very mischievous kid who loved playing in the fields. Paul had taken more after Ookpala as he was also stealthy and sharp in his childhood.

"Paul, it's time!" Ookpala screamed.

"I'm coming, Father!" Paul screamed back.

Paul jumped from a branch and landed right in front of his father. He couldn't stop grinning because he had landed perfectly. Paul kept looking at his father to get acknowledgment from him.

"Great. You didn't break any bones," Ookpala remarked, trying to tease his son.

"Father, I was good this time," Paul insisted.

"Everyone is already at the festival, and you're still here climbing trees."

"I don't like those long speeches, Father," Paul shrugged.

"You have to respect the people you live with, Paul. It means a lot to them. You could go there and dance a little, and then you can come back if you want," Ookpala explained as he tried to humor his son.

"Let's go then."

Prince Ookpala started walking, and Paul ran after him. They reached the ceremony just in time before the festival started. Ookpala left Paul among the children, where Peter was also standing. He then went on to join his wife in the main ceremony.

Iredia was waiting for Ookpala. She didn't want him to miss the speech of the village head. They had been attending the festival together since they arrived at Yola.

"You made it. I thought you were going to miss his speech," Iredia whispered to Ookpala in the crowd.

"Paul," Ookpala said in answer.

"I know. He has been so careless, I get worried for him sometimes," Iredia said.

"He's a fast learner and making the most of it."

"Just like his father," Iredia grinned.

"Ehem," the village's head coughed before starting his speech.

"The Lord Jesus is great. He has brought us all together to thank him for the bountiful harvest. Let's join hands to thank Him for the harvest and produce he has blessed us with this year. May He always be merciful to us. May He protect our village, women, and children...."

"My Prince," a man in a black drape whispered suddenly catching Ookpala's attention.

Ookpala froze, as he was not used to anyone calling him my prince except his wife.

Iredia turned back to see a tall man beside Ookpala, whispering to him. The head's address was still going on, and everyone was busy listening to it. But Ookpala was talking to this strange man who looked out of place and certainly didn't belong to Yola.

"Is everything okay?" Iredia asked her husband, who had wrinkles on his forehead.

"I'll be back. Keep an eye on the kids," Ookpala told Iredia and left with the mysterious man.

Chapter 5: Duty Calls

ESOHA, THE HEAD OF the Benoni guards, drew out a parchment from his robe and handed it to Prince Ookpala.

"How did you find us?" Ookpala asked in a low voice as they walked outside. He was staring at Esoha like he would kick him out of Yola.

"Do you think the Kingdom didn't know about your whereabouts all along?"

"Then why now, Esoha?" Ookpala demanded.

"I'm here to deliver this message," Esoha said with pursed lips.

Ookpala took the parchment out of Esoha's hand and aggressively rolled it down. Ookpala was confused after reading the message. He glared at Esoha. He was in disbelief and couldn't understand why this was happening now.

"What happened to my half-brothers?" Ookpala was almost screaming.

"Your brothers are no more. You're next in line for the throne."

Ookpala's eyes dampened with tears of sorrow.

"How?" he managed to ask.

"Prince Nosa and Uyi, his son, were assassinated by the hands of Princess Aboma before Nosa could be crowned. Oba Osu had been the one on the throne for about seven years until his health failed him."

"Was he in a lot of pain?" Ookpala asked as he tried not to look Esoha in the eyes.

"Sadly, yes. But he was a good Oba. He changed the tradition of burying wives and slaves along with the dead Oba. He refused to marry and declared you his heir. He had to go up against everyone in the Kingdom but stood up for you and your beliefs.

Your brother loved you to death, he did not want to pass on the blood disease trait, and he wanted you to return to Benoni and inherit the crown from him," Esoha told Ookpala, who was still in disbelief.

"It hurts me that my brother Nosa died so many years ago, and I am only now hearing about it. I'm not sure that I'm fit to rule Benoni since I choose to flee from the Kingdom."

"It doesn't matter if you are fit or not. You're the brother of our departed Oba and the next in line for the crown. It is your duty. You cannot leave your people alone. They can't be left to a random Oba's mercy. You have royal blood. Please, you need to return to your people. We need you," Esoha explained to Ookpala.

"My Prince, what's happening?" Iredia asked. She had come outside and was surprised when she saw her husband with tears in his eyes.

"What happened? Please tell me," Iredia asked as she looked at Esoha.

"I'm the Chief Guard of the Oba of Benoni, my Queen," Esoha stated as he bowed to Iredia.

"My what? I'm no queen," Iredia said, flustered. She couldn't understand why Esoha was calling her a queen.

"You are now. You are meant to be the Queen," Esoha said.

"Iredia, my brothers, Nosa and Osu are dead, " Ookpala explained as he looked at Iredia.

"What?"

"They are gone."

"And your husband is next in line for the throne. We need you two to return to Benoni as soon as you can," Esoha continued.

He folded his hands behind his back.

"I'm not going anywhere. Tell them, my Prince," Iredia replied, fighting her urge to break down.

She was getting upset. She had made a home for herself and her family in Yola. She didn't want to go back to Benoni, where people would get killed over the throne. All Iredia wanted was a peaceful life, and it was in Yola.

"Yola is our home," Iredia told Esoha sternly.

"Benoni is your home, My Queen," he replied.

"Why aren't you saying something, My Prince? Why is this man talking to me like that?" Iredia pleaded to Ookpala, who looked lost. He was still shocked after finding out about his brothers' death.

"Are you here alone?" Ookpala finally spoke.

"No. I'm supposed to be your messenger, but I didn't travel all the way here alone," Esoha said.

"Tell everyone with you to wait outside the village," Ookpala told Esoha.

"Whatever you say, my Oba," Esoha bowed and left.

As Ookpala walked outside the field, he saw four horses mounted by men draped in black robes, just like Esoha. Ookpala saw them riding outside of the village and then turned to Iredia.

"Please don't tell me we're leaving Yola," Iredia pleaded with tears. When Esoha bowed to Prince Ookpala and called him "My Oba" without Ookpala contesting the address, she knew what was coming, and she wasn't prepared for it.

"I don't want to return either, my love. But this is a decision I can't take by myself. Yola has given us a new home. We owe a lot to this place," Ookpala explained to Iredia, who looked shaken. "Can you please head home with the children?"

"What are you going to do?" Iredia asked.

"I'm going to talk to the head, Chaga and Efe. I owe them this."

Iredia went to pick up the children and walked back home with the other women from the village whilst Ookpala waited until the head had gotten free from his duties in the ceremony.

"Head Chaga, I need to talk to you about something," Ookpala interrupted him while he was talking to someone.

"I know, my son," he smiled at Ookpala, who was left confused by his reaction.

"We will discuss this later in the evening," Chaga told the man he was talking to.

"Why don't we walk to your hut, Prince Ookpala?" Chaga folded his hands.

"How do you know?"

"I know everything, and I'm not angry," he said.

He was right. Chaga didn't look upset or disturbed as Ookpala had expected him to be. He was calmer than the sunset. They started walking to Ookpala's hut.

"How did you find out?" Ookpala asked.

"I didn't. I always knew. You wouldn't remember this, but I met you when you were merely a child. I used to travel a lot for spiritual journeys. Once, your father sent a message for me."

"What message?"

"He was worried for you. You were the third son, and he had a dream that you would rule the Kingdom. However, third sons do not get to rule in Benoni. He wanted me to anoint you, so I arrived at the palace, and there you were," Chaga explained.

"I was a child then. How did you recognize me when I arrived at Yola?"

"I don't forget the people I anoint. Also, it was destiny. When you were anointed, I gave you the tribal marks beside your left eye. The one chosen from the heart of the King is given specific left-eye tribal markings during their anointing for rulership. No one forgets their anointed crown prince."

"I was the third son. How could my father have known?" Ookpala asked.

"Your father was a believer in Christ. He had the gift of prophecy. Most of his dreams foretold the future."

"My father was a Christian?" Ookpala asked incredulously. "Impossible. I find that very hard to believe. He was a pagan. A staunch idol worshipper. He had sworn to worship god Otun."

"No, he was not. He struggled with his faith, finding it hard to effectively represent it. Unfortunately, he never invested in growing his faith by undertaking the study of and meditation on the Bible, so he remained a spiritual prodigy," Chaga explained.

"However, you and your wife Iredia have accepted Christ. In accepting Christ, you have even renamed your children Peter and Paul. You have been studying the Bible. Your journey is established on the right foundation. The gift of righteousness is fully at work in you. When it's time for you to anoint your successor, your inner witness will notify you."

"Chaga, what should I do now?" Ookpala asked.

"The question is, what do you want to do?"

"I am scared about the traditions of Benoni regarding twins. However, my twins are already seven years old. I believe they have already passed the threshold of danger. Twins are killed at birth in Benoni. I would like you to bless and anoint Peter as my successor. Then, I will want to be at home."

"And where is that home?" Chaga stopped to look into Ookpala's eyes.

"Home used to be Benoni, but those people are cruel. They kill the wives of the Oba when an Oba passes. They kill twins at birth and I have twin sons. They are staunch pagans with idol worship and idol worship festivals! These go against my sense of morality and my Christian beliefs for my future and that of my family. They don't care much about lives or family! All that matters to them is the Obadom. I couldn't bear it if something happened to my family if I were to go back to Benoni!" Ookpala looked frustrated.

"Then why are your eyes damp?" Chaga asked as he wiped the tears from Ookpala's face.

"My brothers are no more. My people need me. They need to be reconciled from their pagan ways. I have a higher calling in Christ to reconcile the unsaved to God. This calling is higher than my personal choices. I am not my own but a servant to Christ. However, I also fear the wrath and hatred of the people. I rejected them and abandoned my duties as a prince after my father died."

"Wasn't your brother the Oba? He decided to pardon and exonerate you. Therefore, it is time you forgive yourself as well and move on. Your brother even named you his successor. The people have already reconciled themselves to you as their Oba's successor. You are a new creation, washed and cleansed by God. You have a higher call to reconcile your people to God, so that they may repent from idol worship. You already know this and you just said it," Chaga raised his eyebrows.

"Prince Osu and Nosa were my family. Nosa should have ruled for a long time but he left the world too early. Even Osu, has joined him. I don't know what will happen to the Kingdom now. I don't know what will happen to my home," Ookpala looked in the distance while speaking.

"Home."

"Pardon me?" Ookpala didn't understand what Chaga was saying.

"You called Benoni home."

Ookpala was shocked.

He didn't even realize that he still considered Benoni his home. But it was the place he grew up. He played in the courtyard of the palace. He went to bed with his father. He grew up with his brothers there. He fell in love there.

"What am I going to tell Iredia?" Ookpala scratched his head.

She wanted a peaceful life and had built a home here. She wasn't going to willingly leave Yola.

"She loves you with all her heart. She will understand."

Chaga and Ookpala finally reached the hut where Ookpala's family lived. Ookpala opened the door to find Iredia gathering their belongings.

"What are you doing?" Ookpala asked Iredia, who appeared like she was in a hurry.

"Preparing for our journey." Iredia replied.

"Iredia, it's your decision as well. I'm not going to ignore your needs and desire for my interests," Ookpala told Iredia.

"My decision is to never live without you. I promised never to question your decisions again. I will go wherever you go. If you're going to walk in the fire, then I'm going to do the same. My place is beside you," Iredia said resolutely as she looked into Ookpala's eyes.

"I promise I will protect you and our children with my life. I will never let anyone harm you. You three are my life."

"And you are ours, My Oba," Iredia embraced Ookpala.

"The children need Chaga's blessing. He's here," Ookpala called in Chaga, who was waiting outside the hut for the couple to decide.

Chaga blessed and anointed Peter and Paul. On Peter, he put identical tribal marks to his father's beside his left eye, signifying that the lineage of the Oba would pass from Prince Ookpala to Peter, should Prince Ookpala cease to be.

"WE NEED TO MEET EFE," Iredia reminded Ookpala.

How could Ookpala forget?

He knew that bidding farewell to Efe would be the hardest part of leaving Yola. He was like a brother to Ookpala. Yola was home because he was there. Efe had left Benoni with him years ago when he and Iredia decided to abandon Benoni.

Ookpala walked to Efe's hut, which wasn't very far from his. He held back his emotions as he bravely went to his home to tell him that he was leaving Yola.

"Efe? Can you come outside?" Ookpala asked.

"Sure. Why didn't you stay back for the festival?"

"That's what I'm here to talk about. My brothers are dead, Efe. I'm next in line for the throne," Ookpala told Efe.

"How did you find out?" Efe's eyes widened.

"People from the Kingdom arrived here to deliver the message."

"People? You said you weren't going to return to Benoni, right?" Efe was sure that Ookpala wasn't going to leave.

"I have decided to leave. I have to take my brother's place as the next Oba, or the Kingdom will fall," Ookpala said, hoping that Efe would understand.

"This can't be true. You must not be serious," Efe was in disbelief.

"I am."

"This is your home. Remember we were going to teach the youth a thing or two about cultivating smart?" Efe reminded him.

"I wish we could have made that dream come true, but for now, my duty is calling for me. I want you to make your dreams come true. I am going to visit to see your farm school someday," Ookpala held Efe's hand.

"Yes, you will visit."

Efe knew at that moment that it was the last time he would see Ookpala. He didn't believe that the Kingdom would ever be able to provide him with the happiness that Yola did.

"Goodbye, my brother," Ookpala warmly embraced Efe.

"No need for that," Efe said. "I am coming with you."

"You are? Thank God. I was hoping you would say that," Ookpala sighed in relief.

"Where you go, I must follow, My Prince. I am your slave, even if you have accorded me more regard than I deserve. Efe wiped tears from the corner of his eyes.

"Efe, you are free today. You do not have to come back with me." Ookpala stretched forth his hand to tap Efe's shoulder.

"Thank you for granting me my freedom, my prince. But, I still choose to go with you," Efe walked towards his hut.

He grabbed his machete, packed his clothes into a wrapper and slung it on his shoulder; then he hurried outside.

" Let us go, I will fetch our horses," Efe said as he sprinted to the horses' stall.

Peter and Paul didn't understand where they were going, but Ookpala told them they would visit their grandparents' place. Paul wasn't willing to let go of Yola. He kept crying as Iredia took him to the guards waiting for them to leave Yola.

Ookpala waved goodbye to Chaga who held back his tears as they left. Chaga knew that they were likely not going to see each other again.

Chapter 6: Bad Omen

OOKPALA'S FAMILY HAD been traveling for almost two months. In the preceding three days, the sky had not relented in its downpour of heavy rain. The clouds roared as if they were about to descend to the ground. The skies were weeping as the family made their way back to Benoni kingdom.

Peter jumped as the thunderstorm shrieked and a lightning bolt hit a tree nearby.

"Why is it so loud?" Peter shivered as he scooted closer to his Mom.

They were all sitting inside a wooden sedan carriage that was raised on the shoulders of the Benoni guards. The children were not used to thunderstorms since Yola mostly hosted sunny weather.

"God has sent rain for us so we can remind ourselves of His power and what would happen to us if we dare to hurt someone," Iredia pulled Peter in for a close cuddle from where he was holding his mother's hand since he was petrified of the loud noise.

"Why would anyone hurt other people, Mother?" Paul asked as he stared at his mother with his doe eyes. "I am not scared. Peter is just a baby!"

Yola was very different from Benoni. People rarely heard of violence or gore, unlike Benoni, where killings were more common after the old Oba took his last breath. Peter and Paul were unaware of what was awaiting them in their father's homeland.

Ookpala was riding his horse alongside the carriage. Drenched from the storm, he slowed down his pace to ride closer. He could hear Peter getting scared, so he grew worried. Ookpala lifted the carriage curtain to talk to Peter, who was shivering every time the clouds roared.

"Peter, my child, we are very close to home. Hang in there," he encouraged.

"We just left home, Father," Peter raised his head from his mother's bosom.

"Father, I am not scared," reiterated Paul with his smile missing his two front teeth.

"That is good. Keep it up. We are close to Benoni." Prince Ookpala looked at Iredia, who had pursed her lips, trying not to say anything that would disturb their son.

Ookpala sighed, looking back at Peter. He was still innocent. He thought they would return to their home in Yola eventually. Little did he know that they had left Yola behind for good. He was probably never going to see the place where he was born again.

Prince Ookpala's clan entered the boundary of Benoni. Ookpala laid his eyes on the place he had once called home. He was the last son of the old Oba. He no longer had any brothers in the Red Palace. Ookpala's mother had been buried with his father a long time ago. The Red Palace didn't seem like home without his parents and his brothers. Ookpala sighed heavily as the horses stopped right before the great gate of the palace.

Esoha dismounted from his horse and spoke to the guards of the Red Palace. A while later, a woman draped in a brown robe stepped out of the great gate. She walked up to Prince Ookpala's horse and even though Ookpala's face was covered by black cloth draped all over his head to hide his face, she still recognized him.

"My Oba."

"Mishkia?"

Prince Ookpala recognized her voice. Mishkia had a very peculiar voice that had a baritone, yet it was soft at the same time. Mishkia was now Chief Maina's wife. She bowed to Ookpala, but he quickly dismounted from his horse and lifted her head.

"You are still as beautiful as ever. You have grown up!" Ookpala joked.

"It's been a while," Mishkia grinned, but it had a hint of sadness.

"The last Oba..." Ookpala began.

"He kept saying your name while he was taking his last breath. He never fostered bitterness towards you. He loved you till he breathed his last," Mishkia looked at the ground as she spoke.

She couldn't look into Ookpala's eyes anymore. He was designated to be the next Oba. As Mishkia spoke to Ookpala, a huge crowd swarmed the great gate of the Red Palace. It was only a matter of minutes till the entire ground was flooded by the people of Benoni.

Before Ookpala could say anything, a swarm of people picked him up and lifted him onto their shoulders.

"Long live, Oba Ookpala!" Esoha's voice echoed among the crowd.

It was still dark as the sun rose gradually. The crowd held torches in their hands as they lifted their next Oba and brought him into the Red Palace. Ookpala tried to raise his voice so people would hear him, but the crowd's noise drowned his voice out.

"Wait, wait, wait!" Ookpala kept screaming at the top of his lungs, but no one was listening to him. Efe made his way through the crowd to reach for Ookpala. He finally made it to him.

"Oba, your family is my responsibility. Don't worry about them. I'll take them to the Old Palace," Efe said.

"No. Please tell them to put me down. My wife would be worried," Ookpala replied.

"Put him down!" Efe screamed, and the crowd stopped moving at once.

Ookpala stood on the ground and started walking back toward the carriage when he saw Iredia moving in his direction.

"My Prince, what is happening?" Iredia asked Ookpala, worried while people stared at their sons who were hiding behind Iredia. Peter and Paul had never seen this many people screaming and roaring. It was very new to them.

"Trust me. Let's go," Ookpala told her. He held Iredia's hand and picked up Peter in his other arm. Iredia picked up Paul, and they started walking to the Red Palace.

When the crowd arrived in the Great Hall, they were asked to wait outside, and only Ookpala, his family, Efe, Mishkia, and Esoha were allowed to go inside. Ookpala entered the Great Hall and saw Chief Maina sitting on a bench in front of the throne that was vacant.

Maina saw Ookpala and then stared at his sons. His stare was so intense that Peter grabbed onto Ookpala's hand, afraid. Paul stared back at Maina boldly. He wasn't afraid of the old man.

"Chief Maina," Ookpala nodded, and so did Iredia.

"Please introduce these children to us," Maina said as he stared at the identical boys.

"These are my sons, Peter and Paul," Ookpala stated. He looked at his identical twin sons and smiled with pride. Ookpala was nervous but he did not show his nervousness. He was aware of the killing of twins at birth in Benori but believed that since his sons were already seven years old, and he was going to be the Oba, he would be exempt.

He thought that Maina would be happy to see his children, but when he looked at him, he found him staring at his boys strangely.

"Are you well?" Ookpala asked, concerned.

"I'm perfectly well. Please escort the children to their chambers, Mishkia," Maina asked.

"As you say," Mishkia responded and reached out for the children, but they backed away.

"She will not hurt you. Please go with her," Ookpala said as he tried to encourage his children, who seemed scared.

"Please escort our queen to her chamber as well," Maina ordered as he looked at Esoha, who nodded.

"Perhaps, she should stay here for a while as we speak about the issues," Efe suggested.

"What sort of issues?" Ookpala asked as he narrowed his eyes at Maina.

"I don't believe the presence of our queen is necessary for this minor issue," Maina said indifferently.

Esoha looked at Iredia and nodded at her. Iredia understood that she was not supposed to refuse Maina's suggestion as he held the highest rank among the chiefs of the Red Palace.

Efe left the Great Hall with Iredia.

"Ookpala, we are all aware that you fled the Kingdom because your wife was pregnant and you were scared of birthing twins. It won't be necessary to recount your history. We need to move forward. But first, I need to ask you something that might be of great concern," Maina began. He folded his hands as he looked into Ookpala's eyes.

"I'm listening," Ookpala nodded.

"Your sons are identical. Are they twins? How come they are still alive?"

"Yes. They were born together. However, they are not newborn twins. They are already seven years old," Ookpala stated. He understood the issue regarding his twin children. They were not killed at birth. The Christian God saved them. "Why is that a concern? You have a problem with seven-year-olds?"

Efe had almost returned to the Great Hall, but he stopped right behind the door when he heard Maina talking about the twins. He came closer, not daring to enter but trying to hide from Maina's sight, which was infamously very sharp and listened to what was being discussed.

"Haven't you been taught about bad omens in Benoni?" Maina asked as he raised his eyebrows at Ookpala.

"I know a few, but they don't matter to me. I have never believed in swearing by bad omens while denying reality. It does not do to dwell on them."

"Well, it was the duty of the old Oba's queen to teach you about bad omens since they hold great significance to the commoners of Benoni," Maina stated, his voice turning stern.

"What does all this have to do with my children?" Ookpala wiped the sweat from his brow. "Look, I already left once, and I can leave again."

He was getting frustrated by all the talk about bad omens.

"Twins are not considered a good omen. You should have known that before bringing your children to Benoni," Maina announced, finally laying the matter out.

"I know. But that is for newborn twins. How can seven-year-old children be bad omens? They are my children and my blood. Iredia gave birth to them. They are perfectly healthy and intelligent as well," Ookpala argued with Maina. "If they leave, then so will I. I wish to have no more arguments about them."

"In that case, I would suggest that you must go back to your chamber as well. You have had a long journey so you must be tired. You should take your rest," Maina stated as he gave a pretentious smile.

Efe finally entered the Great Hall and stood beside Ookpala, who appeared tense and kept looking at Maina.

"Please escort our prince to his chamber. He must rest now. He has a long journey ahead," Maina said to Efe while keeping his eye on Ookpala.

"Shall we go?" Efe asked.

Ookpala walked with Efe to the corridor of the Red Palace. When they left the Great Hall behind, Efe stopped Ookpala and looked at him.

"Your children are in danger, Oba," Efe warned him.

"What are you talking about?" Ookpala asked as he raised his voice.

"Please, lower your voice. They are everywhere," Efe replied as he tried to calm down Ookpala, who was fuming.

Efe glanced around furtively.

"When he said that children are bad omens, he meant it," Efe whispered to Ookpala.

"I know the omens and the traditions. Benoni kills twin babies. My children are not babies! They are already almost seven years old. How do bad omens affect my children?" Ookpala asked, but suddenly, a guard arrived in the corridor where he was standing with Efe.

"Let's keep walking," Efe suggested.

After they were further away from the guard, Efe continued talking.

"The people of Benoni often kill their twins at birth. It is common for people here. You are well aware of this custom." Efe explained to Ookpala as they walked toward the latter's chamber.

"But my children are not newborn babies!! They are seven!" Ookpala sputtered. "Benoni does not kill seven-year-old children; they kill newborn twins."

They finally reached Ookpala's chamber, where Iredia was waiting for him. All the talk about his children and bad omens started bothering Ookpala. He was aware that violence was very common in Benoni, but he didn't expect that his children could be in danger as well because they were no longer babies

"What am I supposed to do now? They won't let me go back to Yola. They took me back from that place," Ookpala asked.

"I will do my best to protect you and your blood, My Oba," Efe promised Ookpala before he went inside his chamber.

"My Prince, let us pray. Our God will keep us safe in this pagan land, Iredia said as she made space for Ookpala to brush by her to his seat.

"You are right, my dear. As always, your wisdom is unparalleled. Let us pray in this Benoni that we came back to. We did not ask for the Lord's guidance together before leaving Yola. Let us pray that he will receive the glory from our return."

"Yes, My Prince," they held hands, and both of them went on their knees to pray concerning their twin sons."

THE NEXT DAY, OOKPALA was informed by Mishkia that he was supposed to attend the council's meeting. As Ookpala got ready for it, he wondered what to do. He did not want to bother Iredia with the entire issue regarding their children. He was aware that Iredia was already skeptical of Benoni and the Kingdom. He didn't want her to worry about their children's safety.

"My Prince," Iredia called Ookpala.

Ookpala was getting dressed by the servants of the palace for the council meeting. He turned back to find his wife approaching him with a long gold tunic embroidered with lions.

"I never imagined I would see you get dressed for the council's meeting. I want you to wear this tunic that belonged to your dear late father. He wore this when he used to rule his kingdom," Iredia beamed.

Ookpala nodded with a grin as Iredia helped him wear the tunic. Ookpala's skin shone against the gold tunic, and he appeared just like his late father did when he was about to meet with the council.

Esoha escorted Ookpala to the Great Hall, where a bench awaited his arrival. As Ookpala entered, he was surprised to see many people sitting on the bench and looking at him.

"Please be seated," Maina asked Ookpala.

Ookpala sat on the seat in the center while he waited for the council to start speaking. Maina cleared his throat and stood up from his seat. "We have come here today to discuss the matter of Prince Ookpala's children. Our Prince is the third son of our beloved Old Oba Eluu, who passed away from old age, seven years ago. This council consists of all the heads of every tribe in Benoni," Maina started speaking. "The matter we are here to discuss is the exile of Prince Ookpala's children-"

"What on earth is this?" Ookpala stood up from his seat. He was fuming with anger. "Exile of children? They are my children, my blood. Why would you send my children away?"

"My Prince," a man called out. He was draped in a green tunic and stood up from his seat. "I'm the head of the Misari tribe, and I speak on behalf of my people. Twins have always been considered a bad omen in Benoni. Their arrival in this world can cause catastrophe and unimaginable chaos. That is the reason why we sacrifice twins when they are born. But the matter of concern here is that your children were born outside Benoni, where our Kingdom doesn't rule. I strongly believe they shouldn't have made it to Benoni in the first pla...”

“Are you suggesting my children should have been killed when they were born?” Ookpala asked fiercely as he cut him off while he was speaking.

“Sacrifice is the word, My Prince,” another man said. He was draped in an orange tunic and stood up. “I'm the head of Fasan's tribe. The people of Benoni will not accept you as their Oba if you are known to be the father of twins. And you are our last hope. You're the last of our Old Oba's lineage, and you must protect the crown even if it means sacrificing your own children.”

“I'm not going to sacrifice my children for the sake of other people or the crown,” Ookpala said sternly.

“The people you speak about are the people you have to rule. How do you expect to rule the Kingdom if your people don't trust you?” Maina asked Ookpala.

“My children will not be exiled at any cost. I will not sacrifice my sons for the sake of unkind people who won't even spare children. I shall not send my children away,” Ookpala insisted. He thumped the bench and left the Great Hall midway through the meeting.

Efe followed Ookpala out of the Great Hall. Ookpala was walking so fast that it was hard for Efe to catch up with him.

“My Prince,” Efe called Ookpala, who kept marching angrily.

“They want me to send my children away. I came back for people like them. I should have never returned to Benoni. People here will never change,” Ookpala fumed. He was furious.

“I understand your anger, and it's justified, but you cannot display your disagreement with the council so strongly. They will come after you if you dare to refuse them,” Efe explained. He tried to make Ookpala understand, though he was not willing to listen anyway.

“Prince Ookpala,” Maina called out. He'd walked outside the Great Hall with Esoha.

Ookpala stopped and looked back at him.

“You have made a grave mistake. You cannot just get up and deny the tradition of Benoni. You must respect how a Kingdom is run if you want to rule it,” Maina thundered. His voice echoed in the corridor while Ookpala kept marching in the opposite direction.

Ookpala stopped and answered just as loudly.

"If that is the case then I will go into exile with my children back to Yola. My family and I will leave Benoni forever. The council can find a new Oba!"

Maina looked at Efe and shrugged.

"Unfortunately, Oba, that is not possible. You are of royal blood. You are here and the throne is vacant. The option is death or the throne. We cannot allow a legitimate heir to roam around to upset the Kingdom in the future should we have a different Oba," Maina stated.

"Prince Ookpala, please think. There is a way. Let us hide the children for now. After you ascend the throne, you can immediately abolish the rule of killing twins and the children will be safe. That way, you and the children will all be alive and well," Esoha suggested as he intervened.

"If that is okay with you, then that is okay with me as well," said Maina.

Ookpala was unsure if he could trust them. He grudgingly agreed. They all made their way back to the council meeting.

"I will need to fast and pray. Ookpala thought to himself. I wish I had done that instead of acting on my feelings when they told me Nosa and Osu were dead. Now, I am already in the midst of this mess. God help me," he prayed as he walked towards his chambers.

"ARE YOU REALLY IN AGREEMENT with hiding the children and abolishing the killing of twins, after the coronation? Esoha asked Chief Maina in private, when they were out of earshot from the prince.

"Dreamers! If Prince Ookpala thinks his twins can live where others have died, he is definitely dreaming," laughed Chief Maina with an evil smirk in his eye.

"I will let you know when." Maina retorted as he spat into the red sand of the red palace.

Chapter 7: The Coronation

PRINCE OOKPALA WAS restless. It had been several days since he'd addressed the council, which gave him a series of sleepless nights. Efe had advised him not to discuss the matter with Iredia since she was already skeptical about coming to Benoni, so this burden was his to bear alone.

"My Oba," Efe called as he knocked on the door of Ookpala's bedchamber.

Efe was standing at the doorstep alongside several men who were carrying machetes and a silver dish in their hands. They kept looking down at their feet and didn't lift their eyes.

"You may enter," Ookpala answered.

Efe entered the bedchamber and saw Ookpala standing beside the window that overlooked the Old Palace. Efe was followed by other men who entered, holding pieces of clothing that were made for Ookpala for his coronation day.

"It's time for you to get dressed, my Oba," Efe told Ookpala, who was still staring out the window. Ookpala turned around and nodded. "Yes, I know, the Priest Ground seclusion awaits."

A lean man holding a gold tunic in his hand stepped forward. Ookpala stretched his arms to let him dress him.

"What's your name?" Ookpala asked.

"Sunday, My Oba," he said while trying not to lift his eyes.

"I'm not your Oba yet. You can look at me like you would look at any other person in the Obadom," Ookpala grinned, trying to ease the tension in the bedchamber.

"You're very kind, my Oba," Sunday responded as he finished tying the tunic around Ookpala with a brown belt made out of cow skin.

Efe stepped forward and hung a long drape over his shoulder that touched his feet. He took a good look at Ookpala before nodding to the men, letting them know that their job was done. They left the bedchamber, leaving Efe alone with Prince Ookpala.

"It's almost time. Do you have any other duties left before leaving for the ceremony?" Efe asked Ookpala.

"I want to see Iredia before I leave," Ookpala told Efe.

"As you say, My Prince."

Efe accompanied Ookpala to the Old Palace, where Iredia was staying after coming to Benoni. Iredia wasn't in the queen's bed chamber as she was supposed to be moved there once Ookpala was crowned.

Ookpala stepped inside Iredia's bedchamber, who was still asleep. He stood at her bedside and brushed her cheek with his hand. Iredia opened her eyes and saw Ookpala smiling at her. She got up immediately.

"My Prince," Iredia said warmly as she embraced Ookpala.

"What do you think?" Ookpala asked.

"You look so unlike yourself, very royal," Iredia finally said after looking at Ookpala's dress for the coronation.

Ookpala grinned and then kissed Iredia on her forehead.

"This is the last time you're going to see your prince," Ookpala said as he looked into Iredia's eyes.

"I don't understand-"

"I'm going to be crowned today. The next time you see me, I will be the Oba of Benoni," Ookpala grinned.

"Be careful with your words. You almost had me worrying about you," Iredia complained as she slapped Ookpala's arm.

"You don't have to worry about anything, my love," Ookpala reassured her as he put his hands on Iredia's shoulder.

"I have something to tell you."

"What is it? You want to leave me?" Ookpala joked as he smirked.

"Someone is going to join us and be a part of our life very soon," Iredia said. She blushed while speaking to Ookpala.

"Who is it?" Ookpala asked, confused.

"I hope it's a girl," she stated instead. Iredia's eyes were filled with playfulness.

Ookpala stood stunned while staring at Iredia. He couldn't believe it. His confused face slowly lit up with a big smile.

"Is it true?" Ookpala asked as he held her hands in his.

"Yes. We're soon going to be a family of five," Iredia grinned.

"Again, you have made me the happiest man. I hope we finally get our princess," Ookpala declared as he pulled Iredia into a warm embrace.

"So do I, My Prince. I cannot wait for our child to be born," Iredia's eyes were getting teary.

"The boys are going to be over the moon when we tell them."

"We'll tell them together after the coronation, My Prince," Iredia stated.

"My Prince, it's time," Efe interrupted them.

He was standing right behind the bedchamber doors, waiting for Ookpala to return.

"I have to leave, my love. Please look after yourself. I will make sure your days are filled with love and joy," Ookpala said as he kissed Iredia's stomach and left her bedchamber.

"My apologies. I didn't intend to intervene, My Prince. We have to leave for the ceremony right now," Efe told Ookpala.

Ookpala walked out of the Old Palace to find Maina and the priests waiting for him to arrive. Maina and Ookpala hadn't been cordial with each other since the council meeting. Ookpala thought it best to maintain his distance from Maina since he didn't want to get into another argument. This was the first time Maina had come to visit him.

"You finally appear like royalty after such a long time," Maina said as he glanced at Ookpala.

"Do I have a choice?" Ookpala responded coldly.

"If only you could understand what you just said."

Efe and Maina escorted Ookpala to the Coronation Ground within the Priest Ground. It was a spacious place made out of red bricks. The guards of the Red Palace guarded the Coronation Ground as well. The guardsmen were wearing their silver flock, which was only meant to be worn during the coronation.

Esoha, the Captain of the Guards, entered the coronation ground and stood beside Maina. He whispered something in Maina's ears and was spotted by Efe. Efe's attention was captured by the ongoing whispering between both of them. Shortly after the whispering, Esoha exited the grounds and went back to the Old Palace.

THE SERVANTS DRESSED Iredia in the Old Palace. She was supposed to wait until the coronation ceremony was over to see her new Oba. She sat in her chambers with two maids and Mishkia.

"Why can't I be present with my husband as he gets crowned, Semar?" Iredia asked the maid who was dressing her.

"It's a tradition carried out for centuries. Women and children are supposed to stay away from the Coronation Ground during the coronation ceremony. The new Oba can't be distracted from performing his duties during the ceremonies," Semar explained to Iredia as she draped her in African print that reached her knees.

"What kind of duties?" Iredia asked out of curiosity.

The woman standing next to Semar turned around to stare at Iredia as if she had committed a sin. Mishkia, the young wife of Chief Maina, was a well-respected lady who attended to the queens and princesses of the Old Palace.

She had risen in rank to Head Palace Keeper after marrying Chief Maina a few years back. The maids all feared her since she had Chief Maina's ear. Mishkia could always be counted on to notice every little mistake and bring it to Maina's knowledge.

"The Oba's duties start from the day he enters the Coronation Ground. He has to sacrifice his desires and pride for the sake of the Obadom. Oba Ookpala will also have to undergo several tests to prove himself worthy of the crown. But what he does inside the Coronation Ground should not concern you," Mishkia said as she shrugged once.

"Why shouldn't it concern me? I'm the wife of Prince Ookpala," Iredia insisted. She felt uncomfortable in Mishkia's presence.

"It's not your duty to know what goes on inside the coronation ground. It is the matter of your husband and the priests present there. We will only receive word once the ceremony is over, but you won't be able to see him for the next seven days."

"Seven days?" Iredia exclaimed. "I heard Oba Osu changed everything."

She was taken aback. She had no idea she wouldn't see Ookpala for such a long time. The thought of not being able to see him made her worried.

"He will be secluded for the next seven days while you stay here," Mishkia reiterated. "Oba Osu changed some things, but not everything," Mishkia walked to the door, scratching her shoulder.

THE ENTIRE COUNCIL was present at the Coronation Ground. They were seated in high seats, looking over the coronation of Prince Ookpala. He was supposed to stand on a pedestal in the center of the Coronation Ground.

High Priest Ohenca approached Ookpala with a silver cup. He was accompanied by several other priests who were standing beneath the pedestal.

He sprayed Ookpala with sacred shrine water.

"I shall ask you now to allow the priests of the coronation to strip you so you can offer yourself to the god Otun in the form you were born in. Our god Otun asks you to be vulnerable, and you must oblige," Ohenca spoke to Ookpala loud enough for everyone in the place to hear.

Ookpala was taken aback. He did not expect that he would have to indulge in self-dedication to an idol god during his coronation ceremony. The ceremony's traditions had been a mysterious secret all his life.

As he contemplated complying with their response, he said a prayer in his heart. He heard a still, small voice whisper to him.

"He that breaks the edge, the serpent will bite."

Ookpala looked around him but could not identify the source of the small whisper. Finally, he nodded his head in consent.

The priests around him took Ookpala's clothes off. He tried not to look Ohenca in the eye and kept his head high. Ohenca signaled with his hand, and several women walked near the pedestal.

Ookpala was further taken aback by these women as they were the only non-masculine presence in the Coronation Ground. There were four women, and each of them stripped naked alongside Ookpala.

"What in hell is this? Ookpala backed away as he gripped his genitals for a little privacy.

Ohenca raised his eyes, staring at the idols of Otun in the shrine, and started mumbling something Ookpala couldn't understand. His voice soon became clear, and everyone could hear what he was speaking.

"As the last heir of the Old Oba Eluu is presented to be crowned the next Oba of Benoni, we offer to Otun, the one god of Benoni, four virgin priestesses. They shall cut our new Oba with their sacred knives so his blood can be offered as a sacrifice of obedience, symbolizing his commitment to god Otun and the crown," Ohenca spoke while looking at the carved idols in the shrine of the Coronation Ground.

Ookpala was unaware of the coronation's customs, making him skeptical of everything happening. Ookpala had accepted Christianity when he was living in Yola. He wasn't prepared to offer himself as part of the religious customs of Benoni to god Otun. All of a sudden, it began to make sense why his father was a supposed Christian. He was more like an idolater.

"Maina, I hope you are aware that I'm a Christian now, which will make it impossible for me to perform these customs you speak of," Ookpala pleaded with Maina, who was standing beside him.

The second in command, the Superior Priest of the Priest Ground, walked up to Ookpala. He was draped in an ivory tunic, and a round pendant was hanging around his neck. He was taller than any man Ookpala had ever seen.

"The Priest Ground's traditions are not meant to be questioned by mere mortals. We are the slave of the gods, and we must perform our duty," he scowled as he looked down at Ookpala.

"But how-"

"Each cut you will bear from the virgin priestesses will embody a blessing by god Otun himself. The council has agreed on you performing all the customs required to crown you as our Oba," the second-in-command spoke before Ookpala could say anything else.

Ohenca stepped forward and stood across from Ookpala. He sprayed him with the sacred water once again.

Ookpala shivered in fearful intimidation, as he lost his courage to stand up for himself in the face of the aging priests of the land.

"It is not the easiest task to earn the cuts from the virgin priestesses. You will have to consummate your connection with god Otun by bedding all the priestesses in order to earn your cut," Ohenca went on. "This will serve as a soul tie and blood connection between you as Oba of Benoni and the god of the Benoni people."

"Consummate?" Ookpala asked incredulously. He couldn't believe what Ohenca was saying.

"You must bed them in front of all of us priests and Otun's shrine to earn a cut from their knife. In this consummation, you are Otun's proxy. This exercise is an age-old tradition of Benoni. It also serves to sire reserve heirs for the throne. It is no big deal, your father did it. All your brothers did it too," Ohenca explained.

Ookpala looked at Efe, standing at a distance from the pedestal where Maina and Ohenca were with Ookpala. Efe shrugged at Ookpala, making him understand that he would have to listen to the priests to get crowned.

Ookpala had a choice to make.

Would he stand for the God he believed in or succumb to the pressures of the traditional priests?

His faith in God was being tested. He heard the still, small voice again whisper to him.

"He that defiles the temple of the Lord, God will destroy."

The ceremony started, and one of the virgin priestesses laid down in front of Ookpala and raised up both her knees while holding a small knife in her hand and looking at the sky.

Ookpala shook his head. Preparing to mount the naked priestess, he heard the whisper in the breeze a third time.

"He who breaketh the edge, the serpent will bite."

Ookpala was startled. He looked around but saw no one. Rather, he heard a clap of thunder, and the skies opened and started raining.

Ookpala felt pressured to obey the priests in the Priest Ground. If he refused them, it would have been considered an act of blasphemy against god Otun and could result in instant death.

"I am scared for my life and that of my family," shivered Ookpala. "Why did I come back to this cursed land? If I refuse now, they will kill me just for knowing the secret of the Priest Ground. What do I do? If I kill myself, I will go to hell. If I do not kill myself or comply, they will kill my children."

Ookpala felt like he had to protect his family from the claws of this traditional council. To Ookpala, his family was first beyond any other considerations.

He wanted to be Oba. He needed to be Oba to abolish the killing of twins and thus protect his twins from being killed.

The ties of the traditions of men on him were stronger than the ties of his faith. Ookpala chose to do exactly what the council commanded; "God help me," he prayed silently as he yielded to their pressure and by doing so, he gave up his faith.

As Ookpala consummated and created a soul tie with god Otun by bedding the priestesses, the entire council watched them and kept chanting. The priestess didn't look into Ookpala's eyes and kept staring at the sky, biting down on a palm frond leaf between her lips continuously.

When Ookpala was finished bedding the priestess, she stood up and rewarded him with a cut from her knife. It was a tribal cut on his chest, between his nipples, deep enough to make him bleed.

One after another, the four virgin priestesses laid down in front of Ookpala so he could consummate. Ookpala received several cuts from each priestess's knife. By the time he had finished bedding the four priestesses, he was bleeding from seven tribal markings on his chest, representing a sevenfold soul tie with the god Otun.

Ookpala's blood was running down his chest when High Priest Ohenca placed a cup beneath the cuts. His blood poured into the cup, and Ohenca left the pedestal with the cup in his hand.

"WE MUST WAIT IN THE Bamboo Room while the ceremony takes place. Semar, please escort the boys while I escort Princess Iredia to the waiting place," Mishkia ordered as she ushered Iredia to walk so she could follow her.

The Bamboo Room was a tall circular sitting room meant to be used only by the queens and the Oba's children. Mishkia asked Iredia to sit inside. Then she called the Old Palace's maids and told them to bring the children. Peter and Paul were brought to the room by Semar, and they ran to hug their mother as soon as they saw her.

"Where is Father?" Peter asked Iredia.

"He is occupied with his duties, my love. Soon your father will rule Benoni, so he will have a lot to do," Iredia told him.

"What does *'rule'* mean?" Paul asked innocently.

"Well-"

"Princess, here is some soup for you and the little princes. It has been cooked specially to entice your taste buds," Semar interrupted them. She approached Iredia with a tray holding three bowls of soup.

"I need to use the outhouse. Will you please feed Peter and Paul while I go and ease myself?" Iredia asked Semar.

Mishkia looked at Semar with stern eyes. Semar nodded at Iredia hesitantly and took the spoon from the tray. Iredia left the Bamboo Room, leaving Peter and Paul alone with the maids.

OHENCA PRAYED WHILE holding the cup that had the blood of Ookpala. He prayed to god Otun. After finishing the prayer, he walked up to the pedestal again and handed the cup to Ookpala.

"You must raise the cocktail of your blood now and swear your loyalty to the god Otun and Benoni. Repeat after me."

Ookpala nodded.

"I shall protect the Obadom of Benoni," Ohenca began narrating, and Ookpala followed.

Ookpala swore his loyalty to the god Otun and the land of Benoni. He agreed to put his life at stake if it was required of him. He swore not to hesitate to sacrifice the lives of the people who betrayed the god Otun and Benoni. He agreed to uphold the traditions of the Obadom before his interests.

Ookpala repeated everything Ohenca narrated to him loud enough for everyone to hear.

"We will move on to swearing your loyalty to the palace now," Ohenca informed Ookpala.

He swore his loyalty to the council of the Red Palace. He agreed to act according to the council's counsel as they only wished well for the Obadom. He consented to put the priests of the Priest Ground on the highest ranks of respect as they spoke for god Otun.

Ookpala glanced at Maina, who was staring at him. He paused for a second while taking his vows for the coronation but then stopped looking at him and resumed. After the vows, High Priest Ohenca walked to the god Otun idols mounted on the shrine, and he sprinkled Ookpala's blood on them, while chanting.

With this blood oath, Ookpala was bound by blood to this idol god Otun.

WHEN IREDIA RETURNED to the Bamboo Room, she saw her sons lying on the ground. It didn't worry her immediately, but then she walked up to them and noticed they were lying unnaturally. She didn't understand why they were sleeping when they were supposed to be eating the soup.

"Didn't they want to eat? Did they fall asleep?" Iredia asked Semar, who was standing at the door.

"I suppose," Semar responded coldly.

Iredia put her hand on Peter's head and suddenly moved away. Peter's forehead was cold. Iredia started touching Peter's neck and chest, and she realized his heart wasn't beating.

"What is happening? It feels like his heart is not beating?" Iredia screamed at Semar fearfully, shocked and surprised.

Iredia saw Paul, and she touched his chest as well. His heart wasn't beating either. She started to scream as the shock and grief of what had happened hit her. It looked like she had lost her mind as she ripped at her hair and her clothes in confusion while howling out her grief. She couldn't understand what was going on. Iredia thought it was a nightmare, except it wasn't.

Her sons were cold! They were dead.

She glanced at the table and noticed the half-eaten bowls of soup.

"Did the soup have something to do with this?" Iredia demanded, but once again, she got no answer.

She got up angrily and shook Semar, who was hanging her head in silence.

"What did you do to my sons? What did I ever do to you??" Iredia screamed as she slapped Semar.

IREDIA'S SCREAMS WERE loud enough for the people outside the Bamboo Room to hear.

"She is alive," Esoha whispered to the other man carrying a machete outside the Bamboo Room.

"Why didn't she have the soup?" the man carrying the machete asked.

Esoha knew what he had to do.

IREDIA WAS CRYING, holding her sons in her arms, but then she heard the clanking of the machetes. The men started rushing towards the Bamboo Room. Iredia thought help was on the way and felt relieved.

Then, she heard Esoha's command.

"Call your men to go after Iredia. She is alive. She needs to be finished right now. We need to give the new Oba an opportunity to start afresh without a queen that reminds him of the Christian God. Esoha ordered the men with machetes.

She knew that she was in danger. Now that Ookpala was not by her side, she felt like she could only rely on herself to get out of this situation.

She stood up and asked Semar to show her a door for exit. Semar stayed silent, still refusing to say anything to her.

"You owe me, Semar," Iredia pleaded through her tears. "My sons are dead because you couldn't protect them. Will you now stand and watch me get ripped to pieces? Where is the back door of this room?"

A silent Mishkia, who had observed the whole happening between Semar and Iredia, pointed at a small door that was hidden behind a table. Iredia ran towards the door and opened it just as she heard footsteps and loud shouting behind her.

She crawled through the door into a hidden tunnel. She closed the door quickly on her way out. It was extremely dark inside, and Iredia couldn't make out anything, but she kept crawling until she saw a ray of light.

The door led to the palace's backyard, which was covered with bushes. She found a tree with sturdy branches. She climbed up to a branch and sat on it. Iredia had escaped with her life.

"Father, help me," a trembling and scared Iredia prayed, while she sat on top of the tree.

Iredia decided to stay on the branch till the assailants stopped chasing her. She kept looking down to keep an eye on the men who were after her. She sobbed in relief as she tried to catch her breath. Suddenly, Iredia gasped when she felt a sharp pain in her leg.

She tried to see what was causing it and saw a snake going down the tree.

A snake. It had bitten her!

Before Iredia could do anything, she lost her grip and fell from the branch. She hit her head on a large stone and lost consciousness immediately.

THE SEARCH FOR IREDIA went on all night until finally, Esoha and his men found her lying on the ground. Iredia was drenched in blood and lying face up on the ground. It was clear to see that she'd been gravely injured.

"She is dead," a man informed Esoha.

"Are you sure?" he tried to confirm.

"Yes. Look here, she has been bitten by a snake, and it looks like she fell from this tree. Only a miracle could have saved her."

"Well, miracles don't happen to the mothers of twins who have a history of influencing a prince to abandon the God of the Kingdom," Esoha responded, leaving Iredia's body behind and heading to the palace.

THE CORONATION CEREMONY had taken an entire day. Ookpala was bleeding continuously and was laid down in a chamber of the Coronation Ground to rest. Efe draped Ookpala in long white fabric. It would get replaced when it got soaked with blood.

"The seclusion period will last for seven days, and you must not leave the premises of the Priest Ground until you have healed properly. Once you are healed and healthy, you will be considered fit to address Benoni as their new Oba," Efe said as he poured water into Ookpala's mouth.

Ookpala was so weak that he started losing vision and passed out.

"He who breaks the edge, the serpent will bite," a voice rang in Ookpala's ears, and he woke up, startled. Ookpala felt as if something wasn't alright. He

opened his eyes and saw two young men wearing white tunics sitting beside him.

"How are my wife and children?" Ookpala asked in a faint voice.

"We are also in seclusion with you, and we don't have any contact with whatever has been going outside the Priest Ground, but everything is all right. You don't need to be worried," one of the young men answered.

"My Oba. You need to have some food," said Efe.

Efe tried to feed Ookpala, who shook his head.

"You need food to heal. You have to be completely healthy," Efe insisted.

Ookpala let Efe feed him. He closed his eyes, trying to pray, but something stopped him from praying. He felt shame, self-condemnation crept up on him, and he couldn't pray.

"He who breaks the edge, the serpent will bite. He who defiles the temple of the lord, God will destroy," the small still voice had changed. The voice was loud and ringing in his head.

EFE HAD BEEN SPOON-feeding Ookpala as he could not get up to eat or drink. Ookpala kept having nightmares. In his nightmare, he was being chased by the idol of god Otun's shrine with a short axe, and he would often mumble in his sleep. Efe was advised by Maina to keep a strict watch on Ookpala, causing him never to leave his side.

After three days, Ookpala started to wake up. He was still weak and fragile. The cuts were bandaged, but he could still feel the pain.

"I don't want to drink this soup anymore," Ookpala told Efe. He turned his face away when Efe tried to make him drink the soup.

"The soup will help you regain some strength," Efe explained to him.

Ookpala had no other option as he wasn't strong enough to walk and couldn't exert any force. He was in a helpless situation. Efe kept spoon-feeding him with the soup.

After seven days of seclusion, Ookpala felt his strength return to him again. He was finally able to get up and walk.

"Congratulations! You have successfully completed the coronation seclusion," Efe said to Ookpala as he praised him and handed him the scabbard for his knife.

OOKPALA WAS ESCORTED back to the Red Palace. As he stepped out of the Coronation Ground, the staff of the Red Palace bowed to him. Ookpala tried to stop them from bowing, but Maina stopped him from doing so.

"You are the Oba now. People are supposed to bow before you. After all, you will rule Benoni and protect their interests," Maina said. His eyes gleamed as he spoke to Ookpala.

"Where is Efe?" Ookpala asked Maina, who was walking beside him.

Maina hesitated before he answered him.

"He went ahead of you to prepare for your return. He is at the Red Palace."

Esoha appeared in front of the gate of the Red Palace. He had an indifferent expression as if he had turned to stone. It was hard to tell his thoughts as he never allowed his face to express his emotions. Mishkia was also standing beside Esoha. Mishkia didn't have her usual buoyant expression. Rather, she looked anxious and could not stop wringing her hands together.

"I wish to see my wife and children," Ookpala said.

He couldn't wait anymore. He had been thinking about his family and wanted nothing more than to see their faces.

"Why don't we walk to your throne first?" Maina suggested.

"I said I want to see my family," Ookpala insisted sternly.

"Will everyone please stay outside for a little while?" Maina requested the people accompanying Ookpala to the Red Palace.

Ookpala was unaware of what had happened while in seclusion, but he sensed something wasn't right. Maina wasn't giving him straight answers. He appeared to be nervous, which was unlike him. Ookpala came inside the Red Palace along with Efe, Mishkia, and Esoha, while everyone else was left to wait outside the gate. Ookpala was beginning to get worried.

Maina's eyes remained on the ground as he stepped toward Ookpala. He had his hands folded behind him and was trying not to look Ookpala in the eye.

"I'm afraid I have to be the bearer of bad news," Maina spoke.

"Are my wife and children fine?" Ookpala asked threateningly.

"None of the men were present in the Old Palace when the incident happened, so we had to rely on the details provided to us by the palace's maids," Maina began to tell Ookpala.

Ookpala clenched his fists. He could tell he was about to hear something unpleasant. It was reported that your wife disappeared overnight from the old palace," Maina said with a sigh.

"Disappeared? My wife? She is pregnant! Where will she go?" stunned Ookpala asked, spreading his hands wide.

"We have no clues." Mishkia bowed her head and took a step back.

"So she has not been searched for? What about my children? Ookpala's eyes were bulging from his sockets, while his fists were clenching and unclenching.

"She left with them, my Oba." Mishkia retreated behind Chief Maina in fear for her personal safety.

Chapter 8: Portuguese Pirate

"WHERE IS CAPTAIN JOAQUIM?" Jimmy asked one of the crew members of the African Queen boat.

"I saw him going down to his quarters," the crew member answered Jimmy.

Jimmy walked to the quarters where Joaquim was standing overlooking a large map.

"If we cross the Mimbak coast-" Joaquim mused aloud.

"Captain, can you spare a minute?" Jimmy interrupted him.

"What is it?" Joaquim growled.

Joaquim was the current captain of the pirate boat *African Queen*. He had always had a keen interest in boats since he was a child, as his father also sailed through oceans to trade in stolen ship cargo. His father's boat was called the *Portugal Queen* in his days.

The Portugal Queen was considered one of the biggest boats back in Portugal, where Joaquim hailed from. Joaquim left to sail at a very young age and fell in love with the sea. He had been a man of the sea ever since.

He was a blond-haired Portuguese with a tall frame and a well-trimmed beard. His face followed a cylindrical shape accompanied by a sharp jawline and bright green eyes. Joaquim scowled at Jimmy. He didn't like being interrupted while he mused about his plans.

"Mishkia wants to see you right now," Jimmy said hesitantly in the Benoni language.

"I see. What is it about?"

Joaquim squinted his eyes.

"She says the matter is urgent."

Joaquim wasn't excited about seeing Mishkia. She had a habit of taking him back to the memories he wanted to bury. But Joaquim couldn't avoid her forever, given the history he shared with Mishkia. She was the person who had once saved his life.

Joaquim had gone into the bushes for nature's call years ago when he met Mishkia for the first time. She was in labor as a very young, unmarried teenage girl. Mishkia's pregnancy was the result of her teenage indiscretion. The father of her child had long disappeared, his whereabouts unknown. Her sister, Lushinna, was by her side during the labor, helpless as to what to do.

Joaquim assisted them with labor and ended up bonding with Lushinna during that delivery experience. The baby was a boy, and they called him Ebere.

Lushinna, Mishkia's sister, was fascinated by geography, which caught Joaquim's attention. Together, they drew a new map of Benoni that would make trade with Benoni easier.

Joaquim was smitten by Lushinna's spirit, which set her apart from everyone else, in his opinion. Eventually, Joaquim and Lushinna married after a short courting period. Joaquim shared a strong bond with Mishkia when his wife was alive. He thought he was the luckiest man, but tragedy awaited them.

Lushinna was pregnant with the couple's first child when pirate slave traders attacked the Portugal Queen. They snuck into the boat, set the boat on fire, killing people as they took control of it.

The slave traders captured the crew. Joaquim was chained as he was made to watch his beloved wife Lushinna get raped by the slave traders. Lushinna went into labor, but no one helped her. They left Joaquim to watch his beloved wife scream in pain of labor right before his eyes.

As fire engulfed the boat, the flames rose in the air, making it visible to people in Red Palace to see it. When the Red Palace's guard spotted the fire, they started to gather so they could rescue people who were onboard the boat.

Mishkia also saw the fire, and when it struck her that it was the Portugal Queen, she ran barefoot out of the Old Palace, worrying for her last sister, who was on the boat.

The guards managed to break Joaquim's chains just in time before the fire reached him. They also carried Lushinna to the palace, but she was unconscious and bleeding. Joaquim ran to check on Lushinna only to find out that she hadn't been able to survive the delivery.

Their newborn child, a son, was lying next to Lushinna. Joaquim held and hugged him to his chest, hoping to hear a heartbeat. One of the palace maids told Joaquim that his son was stillborn. It didn't stop Joaquim from hugging his son until a guard finally had to take the baby away from him for the funeral.

It had been a few years, but Joaquim couldn't let go of his tragic past. He was merely a gentle trader of fabric and animal skins but the brutality he had witnessed nearly killed the kind and charming soul he used to possess.

Joaquim decided to avenge his family and free his captured crew. He repaired his boat. He renamed the boat the African Queen from Portugal Queen.

He turned his life around and made it his mission to rescue slaves. He recruited crew for his boat, and the hunted became the hunter. Subsequently, his crew was entirely made up of slaves who Joaquim rescued.

Soon, Joaquim turned into a slave pirate vigilante who would attack slave boats along with his crew. He would set the chained slaves free and take them far away from their captors. He was a pirate whose only interest was in stealing cargo of slaves from their seafaring captors.

Joaquim's crew respected him more than anything in the world, as they owed their freedom to him. Jimmy was one of Joaquim's earliest crew members whom he had freed from the pirate slavers who had captured him. They would jump in a fire if Joaquim asked them to, as they held him in such high regard.

Captain Joaquim became a slave trader's nightmare. He would set sail and attack slave traders. Joaquim wanted them to suffer the same fate that they sentenced their slaves. Joaquim's crew put slave traders in chains. They sold them to the highest bidders at European slave auctions. The proceeds from these auctions financed his crew.

Joaquim wanted to make sure that slave traders feared his arrival. He didn't leave any stones unturned when turning their nightmares into reality. He was a skilled machete pirate, a feared opponent, and a brutal-fate-awaiting-slave-traders.

Slave traders would hatch strategies to catch him as he was known for hunting them. They kept failing but didn't stop. The war between the African Queen and the slave traders had become a part of folklore and tales narrated to villagers and children alike in Africa.

It had been a long journey that carried on for weeks. Captain Joaquim had returned freed slaves to the border of Benoni. The slaves were about to get moved to the Americas when the African Queen arrived.

The battle between the slave traders and Joaquim's crew caused bloodshed but ended in the liberation of the slaves rescued from the boat.

The African Queen had reached Benoni's port to leave the now-freed slaves in a safe place. The crew had just finished escorting them to Benoni, and Joaquim was preparing to set sail again.

It was how Jimmy yelled Mishkia's name that concerned Joaquim. Joaquim walked with Jimmy to the spot where Mishkia was waiting for him. He saw Mishkia impatiently standing in a corner.

"Mishkia?"

"We need your help," Mishkia said as she rushed to Joaquim. It was when she moved that Joaquim saw she wasn't alone. A woman was lying on the floor, probably unconscious.

"What is happening, and who is this woman? Is she alive?" Joaquim became anxious.

"She is Cleopatra. She is your wife, and she is pregnant," Mishkia told him.

Joaquim was taken aback by this and couldn't understand what was happening. His eyes widened, and he looked at the unconscious woman and then at Mishkia.

A SHUDDER PASSED THROUGH the boat, jerking the sleeping Captain Joaquim awake from his afternoon slumber. Joaquim was reminiscing about his past and dreaming all the while.

It was a dream mixed with some of his memories. But it seemed too real. It took Joaquim some moments to return to reality.

"Who? Why did that woman seem so familiar?" Joaquim asked himself.

"Captain! Captain!" Jimmy was yelling.

Joaquim wore his tunic and a coat made out of leather. He moved the curtains of his small cabin and was met with bright sunlight. He tried to shield his deep green eyes with his hands when Jimmy ran in his direction.

"Where is the fire?" Joaquim asked.

"Mishkia is here to see you," Jimmy told Joaquim.

Joaquim paused for a moment. It was strange. He had just dreamed about Mishkia, and now she was here.

"It must be a coincidence," Joaquim thought out loud.

"Coincidence?" Jimmy squinted his eyes.

"Never mind. What happened?"

"It is urgent."

"How urgent?"

"She is not alone."

"What do you mean she is not alone?"

Joaquim started to get concerned.

"She has brought a woman who is unconscious."

Jimmy's words startled Joaquim. He thought he was still dreaming, so he touched the curtains to ensure he was awake.

"Captain, you need to come," Jimmy tried to get Joaquim's attention, who appeared lost.

JOAQUIM SAW MISHKIA; she was standing at the precise spot, just like in his dream. He saw a very weakened woman lying on the floor. He was beyond shocked, but deep down in his heart, he knew what he had to do.

"Joaquim-"

"Is she the one who needs to be rescued?"

Joaquim cut off Mishkia.

"Yes, but how do you know?" Mishkia wondered aloud.

"She is pregnant. You will need to be very careful. Everyone in Benoni is after her life. She is the Queen of Benoni. Wife to Oba Ookpala," Mishkia warned Joaquim.

Joaquim nodded and picked up the semi-conscious woman in his arms. He looked at her face. She was ebony black, her skin was shiny her hair was naturally curly. It was parked in large knots and decorated with royal beads. Her frame was slim and taut. It was obvious that she was a tall woman. She was bleeding, her eyes were shut and her face was completely pale. Her abdomen had a slight roundness to it. She was the most beautiful and nubile female that he had ever laid eyes on.

Joaquim felt close to her, as if he had known her for a long time. He might not have been able to save his late wife, but perhaps he had a chance to save this woman.

"What's her name?" Jimmy asked.

" Her name is Iredia, and she is the Queen of Benoni. Wife to Oba Ookpala, but she will need a new name," whispered Mishkia. "She has to hide, or they will kill her."

"Cleopatra," Joaquim responded. "Her name will be Cleopatra. No one will suspect her true identity with that name."

" Where is your ship's doctor? Queen Iredia was bitten by a snake and fell from a tree. I gave her the anti-venom medicine that Dr. Anita gave me when the snake bit me in the Old Palace's garden that one time.

"No problem, I will get her," Captain Joaquim looked at Jimmy and gestured with his head. Jimmy left the room in search of the doctor.

Mishkia got off the boat, and the African Queen set sail.

Joaquim asked the crew to ready a special chamber for Cleopatra as she was very weak.

Cleopatra sagged like a rag doll, unable to support her legs, and in a daze, Captain Joaquim swung her off the floor into his sturdy arms and strode into the captain's quarters.

She was not speaking. Dr. Anita, Jimmy's wife, came into Captain Joaquim's chambers. She immediately assessed the situation and took over her care from Joaquim.

Chapter 9: The Serpent's Bite

MISHKIA, WHO IS RESPONSIBLE for the palace maids, informed me that your wife was worried about you. Everyone tried to make her understand that you were in seclusion after the coronation ceremony, but she didn't believe anyone. She thought you were dead. When you didn't return for the next three days, her fear started turning into delusion. She escaped in the middle of the night and managed to elope undetected," Maina explained.

"It can't be possible. You're lying! What about my sons?"

Ookpala was in denial. He was furious and shocked. He didn't know if he could believe Maina.

"She left with them. Well, I can call upon Mishkia and the other maids to confirm the events of the night she disappeared. Remember, I was not here either. I was with you at the Coronation Ground," Maina offered.

Mishkia was called to see Oba Ookpala along with the maids of the Old Palace.

"Will you please explain what happened with Oba Ookpala's wife?" Maina asked his wife, Mishkia.

"She lost her senses. We tried to make her see the truth, but she didn't want to believe us. She kept fearing for you and your sons' life. One night she and your sons escaped from the palace along with jewelry and other valuables of Old Palace," Mishkia reported.

Maina hid his smile. He was pleased with his wife. She didn't hesitate once before lying to Oba Ookpala.

"You may go," Ookpala ordered Mishkia. Then he turned to Esoha. "I want everyone in the palace to start searching for my wife and children!"

"The Obadom has many affairs to manage as of now. You're the new Oba, and we will have to arrange matters regarding Benoni that had been put on hold while you were absent. Everyone in the palace cannot be put on this task. We can ask the guards of the Old Palace to start a search party for your family," Maina interjected.

"I said, I want *everyone* to look for my family. What part of my order did you not understand?" Ookpala questioned Maina as he grinded his teeth furiously.

"May I offer my suggestion, my Oba?" Maina interrupted.

"You may not," Ookpala snapped.

He shut off Maina without even looking at him.

Ookpala was devastated. He'd been expecting to see his Queen and children after the seclusion. He didn't have any idea what was happening outside of the coronation ground when he was isolated from the world.

"All of you have made a grave mistake while I was in the Priest Ground. It was your job to look after my family, and you have failed me!" he said aloud.

Efe tried to console him.

"My Oba, I can fathom what you might be feeling..."

"No, *you* cannot fathom what *I* am feeling," Ookpala stated through clenched teeth as he glared daggers at Efe. "You weren't the one who lost his family. I have no idea where my children and wife are. She is pregnant! I don't know if they're safe or have fallen prey to danger. I care for nothing more than their safety. I want every guard and soldier in Benoni to start looking for Iredia and my children!"

Ookpala's voice echoed in the Red Palace. The maids flinched, and everyone bowed their heads.

"As you command, my Oba," Esoha agreed as he bowed deeply to Ookpala, and so did Maina.

"I also want our best soldiers to leave for Yola immediately and the neighboring cities. Now stop staring blankly at me like imbeciles and leave me alone!" Ookpala yelled.

Esoha, Maina, Efe, and the staff complied. They could see that Ookpala was extremely furious and wanted to be alone. As soon as they left, Ookpala sank to the floor, holding his face in his hands. He didn't even want to imagine what might have happened to Iredia and their children. He feared the worst. He refused to believe that Iredia could have abandoned him.

He agreed to become Oba because he wanted to save his family, and now he had lost them. He remembered the warnings of the small voice during the coronation ceremony, and he broke into heart-wrenching sobs.

"As Ookpala sobbed, he tried to pray, but for some strange reason, he could not. "I just feel so unworthy!" he thought to himself. "How can I pray to a God I abandoned in the Priest's Ground? He warned me, that if I break the edge, the serpent will bite, but I disregarded his warning. Now it's too late." Ookpala sobbed in guilt and pain.

Chapter 10: The Night Slave

JOAQUIM DEDICATED HIS time to nursing Cleopatra. He spoon-fed her. Jimmy had never seen Joaquim being so tender with anyone. He wondered what bonded him to her.

Joaquim prayed that Cleopatra would recover her broken spirit and she'd thrive. She was so silent, not speaking, just obedient in doing whatever was asked of her. Cleopatra just routinely stared into space.

"Such beauty," Joaquim thought to himself. He could not help but gaze at her spotless dark skin. Her neck was smooth and long like a gazelle's.

"I wonder why my heart skips every time she looks at me! Her eyes seem so piercing."

He had never been someone who prayed regularly, but he did that for Cleopatra.

Anita, the boat's Portuguese physician, and wife to Jimmy, had been trying to heal Cleopatra's wounds tirelessly. She had barely slept in days. Joaquim had strictly told her not to leave the chamber until Cleopatra was in a stable condition. She hadn't even seen sunlight for a while as she kept treating Cleopatra.

Captain Joaquim entered the chamber as he usually did to check up on Cleopatra. She was still in a daze, but her wounds had started healing.

"How is she doing now?" Joaquim asked Anita.

"She has come a long way since she came aboard the boat. She is stable but still dazed. She must have gone through a horrific trauma and a seizure somewhere."

Captain Joaquim sat beside Cleopatra's bedside. He looked at her face, as she kept staring vacantly, like she was a zombie. She was awake but absent. When she slept, she sweated and thrashed in her bed as she experienced nightmares that she could not voice.

"You're one of the most skilled doctors in Portugal, Anita. That's the reason I decided to bring you onboard the boat. You deserve to be a part of the African Queen. I can see that you have made huge efforts to heal her, but I want to know when will she wake up from her daze?" Joaquim asked hopelessly.

"I'm afraid I don't have the answer to your question. Only God knows when she will awaken. Please know that I'm trying my best here, and I will keep trying," Anita reassured him.

Cleopatra started shivering suddenly. She twitched and jumped, which startled Joaquim. He didn't know what was happening.

"What's wrong with her?" Joaquim asked worriedly.

"She has been having terrible nightmares. We can't do anything about it since she has retreated into herself and is not speaking."

Joaquim felt helpless. He wanted to take her pain away in any way he could. He couldn't bear to see her suffer. Joaquim held Cleopatra's hand and caressed it.

"I am going to bring you back," Joaquim whispered. "Anita, you should take a walk outside. You have been here for a while. You deserve a break."

Gladly, Anita stepped out of the chamber, and the first person she saw was Jimmy, her husband.

"Jimmy, my husband, I greet you," Anita hailed him.

"Oh, you're here. How is she doing?"

"She is better than when she was first brought here, but I can't tell what's going to happen now."

"The Captain seems to have grown fond of her. It's strange that she is not even speaking or interacting with him, but he acts as if he has known her for a long time," Jimmy said.

"It appears to me that they have a strange connection beyond our interpretation."

OOKPALA REFUSED TO have any audience.

It had been months since Iredia had gone missing along with their children. He rarely slept. He was afraid to sleep. In his dreams, he was often tormented by the god Otun, a dwarf wielding an axe, chasing him till he awoke.

In his dream, he could not run very fast. He was laden with multiple chairs. From time, to time, after god Otun got tired of the game of chasing him, he would jerk his chain and trip him to fall on his face.

Ookpala would often wake up in the middle of the night and start screaming Iredia's name, breaking down in sobs.

"Efe!" Ookpala screamed.

Efe ran into Ookpala's chamber. It was the middle of the night, and he knew that Ookpala had woken up from a nightmare again. It was well-known in Benoni that their Oba had started to lose his mind. Efe had started sleeping in Ookpala's antechamber to readily attend to him at night.

"Where are they?" he asked him, pleading through his tears. "Since the coronation ceremony, I have not been myself. What did I tie my soul to? For what? For who? Where is my family? The throne is empty. My life is empty! The God I left Yola with did not step foot in Benoni!"

Ookpala broke down sobbing.

"My Oba, they are not here," Efe consoled him. "I have told you we have been looking for months, but we couldn't find any trace of them."

Efe had to keep reminding Ookpala that the soldiers had been trying to find his family for the past few months. The search for the children and Iredia failed to yield any results.

"When will she return, Efe? When will my children return?" Ookpala asked desperately as he held Efe's hand.

"I'm sure wherever they are, they're fine," Efe tried again to console Ookpala, who seemed to be on the verge of completely losing his mind.

It was difficult for Efe to see Ookpala in that condition. Efe believed that the Oba's family had been killed because of the twins' issue, but he knew he could never tell his Oba his suspicions.

He had to keep lying to him to keep him sane.

Chapter 11: Another African Prince

MONTHS PASSED, AND Joaquim spent endless nights holding Cleopatra's hand and cooling her head with a washcloth while she had her nightmares.

Cleopatra gradually recovered more of her sense but still refused to talk. She silently followed Joaquim's commands without speaking. Her pregnancy drew on and her belly grew. Joaquim never gave up on hoping she would be whole again one day. He wanted to believe in miracles once again. He had been nursing and talking to her for a long time but never felt hopeless.

Joaquim could feel Cleopatra's eyes following him everywhere he went while he was in her room. She seemed to calm down whenever he was close to her.

He could feel the tension building inside him, as his heart raced whenever he was close to her. There were no words spoken between them, but their interactions were subtly changing.

As Joaquim brushed Cleopatra's beautiful, long black natural hair, she leaned her head back onto his wide chest. She reached for his hand and put it on her pregnant stomach.

As he felt the baby kick him from her womb, Joaquim and Cleopatra, shared a glance. It was pregnant with possibilities and he realized something.

"How would I ever let her go?" He rationalized to himself. He had never heard what she sounded like, but she had become dear to him, and he didn't want to lose her. Her proximity made his heart race, and he loved that feeling.

The African Queen docked at a port where it was supposed to get supplies for the boat. Everyone got off the boat except for Joaquim. He stayed with Cleopatra.

After a few hours, Jimmy came back and asked to see him.

"May I come inside?"

"Yes," Joaquim answered.

"I have news. My spy in the city has let me know that a boat has set sail to transport slaves. They have a large cargo of slaves headed to the East."

"Good. Did you manage to get all the supplies?" Joaquim inquired.

"Yes. Should we head in the boat's direction?"

"We need to set sail immediately if we want to catch them before they offload the boat."

"I agree," Jimmy nodded.

"But be careful this time. I don't want any mistakes that could put Cleopatra's life in danger," Joaquim reached for some fruit for Cleopatra.

"HERE WE GOOO, ON THE African Queen. Here we gooo, fighting the evil, here we gooo! Here we go, oh, oh oh—"La-la—la——Here we go,—-—" Jimmy sang along with the African Queen's boat crew.

They had just left the shore of San Bernan, where they had sold the captors of St. Mary, the boat they had attacked. Captain Joaquim and his crew of fighters had successfully captured St. Mary and rescued the cargo of slaves.

Anita and Jimmy danced throughout the entire night. It was a big victory for the African Queen. They executed their plan effortlessly and managed to capture the boat without getting any crew members killed during the battle.

Suddenly, Anita heard screams coming from Cleopatra's chamber.

"Did you hear that?" Anita asked Jimmy.

"Yes, is Cleopatra screaming? That would be a miracle. I have never heard her voice."

Cleopatra had been sleepwalking for five months in a zombie-like daze, with her only sign of recovery being the moments she randomly shared with Joaquim. Anita ran to Cleopatra's chamber, and what she saw shocked her to her core. Cleopatra was sitting on her bed and looking around. Her eyes were aware! She was present at the moment.

"Where am I?" she screamed at Anita in Portuguese. Anita was astonished! The crew has all been speaking in Portuguese these months, and Cleopatra, who had been silent all this while, had apparently been learning their language!

She was speaking!

Joaquim also ran in as he had heard the commotion. He came inside the chamber to find Cleopatra screaming in Portuguese.

"I cannot believe this. You're finally awake!" Joaquim exclaimed. He couldn't believe his eyes or his ears.

"Who are you people, and where am I?" Cleopatra asked.

"Don't you remember?" Joaquim hedged.

"No, I don't. I cannot remember anything," she said. "What's my name?"

"You do not remember your name? Do you remember anything?" Anita stole a glance at Joaquim.

"No, I don't. All I remember is Joaquim caring for me with so much love."

"You have amnesia. I cannot tell you how long it will last, but we will care for you as long as it lasts," Anita started.

"Your name is Cleopatra." Joaquim signaled Anita to leave the room, but Anita remained.

"You are my husband?" Cleopatra looked deeply into Joaquim's eyes.

Joaquim hesitated, then replied, "Yes, I am your husband. Do you remember me?

"Ohh my husband, I cannot remember what happened to me. Please tell me" Cleopatra made a quick grab for Joaquim's hand.

"You are on our boat, the African Queen. I named it after you. We live on our boat. We engage in trade between ports.

"You were raped and injured in a raid, and I have been nursing you ever since."

Cleopatra stared at Joaquim in shock, then stared at her obvious pregnancy.

"We found it difficult to have a child," Joaquim explained. "You got pregnant from the rape. I am not the biological father of your child, but I do not mind being the father of our baby, if you will let me. I love you and I am happy you are back with me."

Cleopatra could not remember her marriage or being raped. She figured that Joaquim must be telling the truth, but she couldn't recognize where she was. Nothing seemed familiar to her.

"I don't understand. Why can't I remember anything?" Cleopatra asked, clearly distraught.

"You have been in a sleep-walking daze for more than six months, my dear. It damaged your health gravely. You're fine. Everything is going to be okay. The important thing is that you are well and awake," Joaquim reassured her as he sat beside Cleopatra and took her hand. "You have fought your injuries bravely, my love. Soon, we will have a child, and our family will be complete."

Anita was shocked at Joaquim's lies but chose to keep silent. Maybe the lies would keep Cleopatra calm for now, she thought.

Joaquim put his hand on Cleopatra's belly. She could see the love he had for her in his eyes. She let him embrace her but still wondered about what had happened to her. She could not remember a single thing.

AFTER A WHILE, CLEOPATRA regained her strength with the help of Anita, whom she had gotten very close to. Joaquim took care of Cleopatra all the time and wouldn't leave her alone. He loved her to death and could have done anything for her.

Cleopatra had also grown fond of Joaquim. She believed that he was indeed her husband and they were going to have their first child. She was sad that she was raped, but she was happy with Joaquim and his crew. A few weeks later, Cleopatra gave birth to a healthy baby boy.

She was shocked when she saw the dark skin of her child. She worried about Joaquim's response, as Joaquim was white European, and the baby was obviously full-blood African. She felt sad, that she could not remember the rape that had fathered her baby.

"Isn't he beautiful?" Cleopatra asked tentatively, raising her eye for Joaquim's reaction, who had tears in his eyes.

"Yes. He is perfect."

"You do not mind that he is African?" she asked.

"No, I do not mind," responded Joaquim. "I am happy I have a son. I only wish to name him Pedro, after my late father."

"Whatever you want, my love," Cleopatra agreed eagerly.

"Your mother is a brave woman. She fought for her life and kept you alive. Here you are. Welcome to the world," Joaquim said while holding his newborn African prince.

"Welcome to the world, Pedro," Cleopatra chuckled as she kissed him on his forehead.

The African Queen held a celebration for the arrival of Joaquim's son. Everyone danced their hearts out and drank late into the night. There were thumps of loud drums as the crew danced.

Joaquim was sitting with Jimmy and Anita. They were having their third glass of rum. They were heavily drunk and were talking about random subjects when the conversation turned to Cleopatra.

"Are we ever going to tell Cleopatra the truth?" Jimmy asked.

"What truth?" Joaquim grumbled. He was too drunk to understand what was being said.

"About her origins," Anita clarified. "About where she came from."

"No. I am happy for the first time in a long while. I have the blessing of having a beautiful woman like her and a child too. I don't want to risk it by revealing the truth to her."

"But isn't it the same as enslaving her? We are on a mission of liberating slaves, then why are we doing the same by keeping her in the dark?" Anita asked. She was concerned. "Cleopatra deserves to know the truth."

"I love her, Anita. I will die if I lose her," Joaquim said as he instantly sobered up.

"Then why would you tell her she was raped?" Anita asked. "Hasn't she suffered enough that you must push this on her too?"

"How else was I going to explain to her why we were having an African baby?" Joaquim responded.

Anita shook her head, not wanting to continue the conversation anymore.

"What you are doing is not right, Joaquim, but we understand. She will never find out about her origins from us, if that's what you want," Jimmy assured Joaquim while looking straight into his wife's eyes.

Sighing, Anita nodded solemnly in agreement.

Chapter 12: He is not my Son

ESOHA'S WATCHFUL EYES accompanied Efe everywhere. He followed him whenever he went to meet Oba Ookpala.

"My Oba, the council is ready to be addressed," Efe informed Ookpala, who had been occupying himself with ancient texts and scripts of the Obadom's ancestry.

Ookpala was aware that the council was once again going to enforce the importance of marrying a woman from a noble house to sire heirs for himself and the throne. He couldn't bear to entertain the thought of exchanging vows with another woman. Ookpala's heart still ached for Iredia, and he wasn't ready to give up on the hope of finding her one day.

Efe accompanied Ookpala to the hall where the council was supposed to meet. When they entered the hall, he saw the familiar faces of the chiefs of the noble clans in Benoni. They had been sending word to Ookpala through Maina to convince him to accept a match with one of their daughters.

"My Oba, you must remember Chief Odunsi. His ancestry goes back to the warriors who fought at the front of the Oyo War. He is the Chief of the Mukira clan and wishes to propose a suggestion that will benefit both you and our Obadom," Maina said as he made a decent attempt at reintroducing the matter to Ookpala, who was already aware of it.

"I value your time and the honor you have bestowed upon the Obadom by proposing your suggestion, Chief. But please be mindful that I have made it very clear to my council that I don't wish to remarry anyone. I am a married man and will remain one until I witness the remains of my Queen," Ookpala stated firmly as he finished the conversation before it started.

Maina stared angrily at Ookpala, who had once again caused the council distress. Chief Odunsi thought it better to be seated back as he didn't want to be stripped of his dignity by dragging the matter of the proposal in front of the man who had given up on the prospect of remarrying.

Soon Odunsi and the other chiefs left the room, and the hall was haunted by the silent and angry stares of the council, which were all set on Ookpala.

"My Oba, there is another matter that requires your attention, and I hope you take it well this time as it can cause great loss to the Obadom," Maina stated as he pressed his point.

"You may begin," Ookpala said.

"It has been seven years since one of the virgin priestesses you mated with during your coronation gave birth to your son, Omonoma. When do you plan to acknowledge him as your son and heir?" Maina asked.

Ookpala was indifferent to the news. He had been notified of this son seven years ago, but he could not be bothered to care about him. He despised the memory of his coronation as it was the same time his wife, Iredia, ran away from the palace. He didn't even think twice about the priestesses he had previously bedded.

"I will not be acknowledging him as anything," Ookpala stated firmly. "He is an abominable seed, the son of god Otun and no son of mine."

Ookpala regretted having participated in the act that still made no sense to him. All it had done was turn him unfaithful to Iredia and cost him his faith in the one true God. He wanted to bury the remaining fragments of that bitter memory, but reality was now looking at him in the eye.

Yet, he refused to acknowledge the truth.

"Since the priestess gave birth to a son, he will be the rightful heir to you and the Crown," Maina pointed out.

"Why?" Ookpala asked icily.

"Since we have not been able to locate Queen Iredia and your twin sons, there must be an heir for the throne."

"I will never accept that child's legitimacy! I only bedded the women because I felt pressured and was too weak to say no. I was manipulated into committing that heinous sin by the stupid shroud of secrecy surrounding the coronation ceremony!" Ookpala roared angrily.

"The Obadom needs an heir," Maina still insisted, unfazed by all that Ookpala had said. "We require a son to succeed you, but that won't be possible until you decide to marry a noblewoman. It has been seven years! Here, we have an opportunity to have an heir. Acknowledge Omonoma! It doesn't matter that the priestess is not your wife, but the child is yours and..."

Ookpala got up and left the council before Maina could finish his sentence.

He could not help flashing back to how, nine months after his coronation, one of the priestesses had died during childbirth, giving birth to his son. The son was subsequently placed with Maina's family, so Mishkia, Maina's wife, who was nursing a newborn son at that time, had also nursed the illegitimate prince.

When Ookpala refused to name the prince, Maina named him Omonoma.

Maina tried to convince Ookpala that the birth of a son had saved his succession, yet he refused to be convinced. Ookpala had always been stubborn, and it didn't seem to get better. Ookpala adamantly refused to acknowledge him and called Omonoma an abominable seed.

Seven years had passed, but Ookpala's heart never softened for his illegitimate son. He didn't wish to amend ties with his heir, and it bothered the council, who had been overjoyed when Omonoma was born.

IT HAD BEEN SEVEN YEARS, and Cleopatra still couldn't recall any memory from the past. She could not remember being raped or her life before she woke up in the boat, pregnant.

She blamed it on the trauma of the rape incident and decided that it was simply because she was not trying to recall the details of such a traumatic event anymore. She found Joaquim's love and Pedro's presence in her life to be enough for her.

She loved the African Queen too. It was her home, and she felt like she belonged by Joaquim's side. Cleopatra had joined the cause of the African Queen to fight slave traders. She started practicing swordsmanship shortly after giving birth to Pedro. Jimmy had taught her to use sharp blades and a machete to defeat her enemies.

Joaquim himself trained Cleopatra for the battles they were going to fight. He didn't want his wife to be as helpless as his late wife had been. He wanted Cleopatra to gain her own strength and stand her ground. She had become an active warrior alongside the boat crew under Joaquim's tutelage.

Joaquim had just returned to the boat with his seven-year-old son, Pedro, after catching a fish he had been trying to hunt for a while.

"My love," Joaquim called out as he peeked inside their shared chamber, but he couldn't find Cleopatra there. Although it had been years since he'd found Cleopatra, his heart still skipped a beat when he couldn't find her. She was too precious to him.

"You're back," Joaquim heard Cleopatra's voice from behind. He turned around to find her holding a jar.

"I was preparing the special spice for the fish. I know how much Pedro likes it to be fresh," Cleopatra said. Her face lit up as she glanced at Pedro, who had come in with his father.

"Why do you look stressed?" Cleopatra wondered as she saw his wrinkled forehead.

"I'm not. I just couldn't find you for a minute, and my heart became restless," Joaquim explained as he kissed Cleopatra's soft but firm hands.

"You need to stop worrying and start helping me prepare condiments for the main course tonight," Cleopatra grinned, making Joaquim smile as well.

"Mother, see, I caught the fish!" Pedro boasted.

"Let's get on to the mission of cooking this delicious and fresh fish you hunted with your father," Cleopatra responded, and Joaquim grabbed hold of Cleopatra's hand as they headed to the boat's galley.

Although Cleopatra couldn't recall the memories from her past, her nightmares never stopped chasing her.

The nightmares were all very similar. She dreamed of two young boys laughing and playing, and then they were dead. Cleopatra would get startled when she woke up from the nightmare. She would be thirsty and scared. The faces of the boys were usually obscured in the dream such that she could not recognize them.

Joaquim used to witness her trembling during her nightmares and would ask her about the matter, yet she tried to avoid the subject by telling him that she couldn't remember anything.

Cleopatra kept wondering why she kept dreaming of those two boys. Their faces were so familiar as if she had known them closely.

She felt a strong bond with the children, and when she found them dead in the nightmare, she felt as if a part of her body had been ripped out from her. She could never remember their faces on awakening, as they would vanish before she could remember them.

Chapter 13: Pedro's Heifer

MUCH TO THE COUNCIL'S disappointment, Oba Ookpala never gave up on his mission to find his wife and sons. He traveled to distant regions accompanied by Efe to search for his family.

"I have spent the last sixteen years searching for my family to no avail. Iredia, how could you just leave me like that? Ookpala thought to himself.

Ookpala was no longer the person he used to be. Everything he had loved, he had lost. He didn't have any hope left to rebuild his life. Ookpala spent his days alone in his bedchamber, forlorn and lonely.

There was no peace left in the ancient texts as well. He was tormented by voices in his head that would echo when he was alone. He was tormented in his sleep by his nightmares. He couldn't escape them. His mind was haunted.

"He who breaks the edge, the serpent will bite. He who defiles the temple of the Lord, God will destroy," the voice haunted him every now and then.

Ookpala found it hard to sleep. His sleep was tormented by god Otun. He constantly dreamt of the shrine at the Priest's Ground. He had long been caught and held in chains at the shrine guarded day and night in his nightmares by god Otun."

He spent countless nights staying up, staring into the vastness beyond the palace. Time had frozen for him. He could no longer move forward.

"Efe, I think I never left the Priest Ground. My spirit is imprisoned there. It is held hostage by god Otun." Ookpala confided in his friend and aide.

Efe was disheartened at seeing Ookpala's state. He did not believe him anymore. He tried to knock some sense into him by trying to stress the importance of stepping out of his bedchamber and managing the Obadom's affairs. All to no avail.

"Why don't you pray to your God? Efe asked. If he is really as good as you say, he will not leave you."

"I have tried. But my lips are just so heavy. Whenever I try to say the words for some strange reason, I just cannot get them out. I feel like my world is locked-up inside me. I asked men to get Chaga from Yola, thinking maybe he could help. But Chaga of Yola has died. I need help. I need my family. I am a slave to god Otun, yet I am Oba," Ookpala sobbed as Efe patted his shoulder.

"OBA OOKPALA HAS REQUESTED your presence in his chambers," one of the chamber guards informed Efe.

It was two hours past midnight. Efe couldn't understand the reason behind this abrupt call. He went straight to the chambers to find Ookpala marching in circles before his bed.

"Efe, call a council meeting in an hour," Ookpala stated. His tone alarmed Efe.

He sounded determined. It seemed like it was a matter of great urgency, but given Ookpala's state of mind, Efe thought it was wise to ask him why he wanted to address the council at this hour.

"I have wasted enough time already, and I don't want to keep repeating my mistakes again. People like Maina have committed or contributed to sins for a long time. I want them to cease these malicious activities at once," Ookpala stressed with great importance.

Efe nodded. He told the guards to inform the councilmen to ready themselves for the address. People were woken up a few hours before the morning sun dawned. Maina was irritated by the Ookpala's abrupt order. He whispered something under his breath before settling in his seat.

"I want every person seated here to listen to me carefully and take my word as the final warning," Ookpala began his address.

Maina stared at Esoha. He was starting to get concerned about the nature of the meeting. Ookpala looked furious and determined at the same time.

Maina and Esoha had been controlling all political matters, while Ookpala had drowned in his sorrows about his lost wife and children. Maina was aware of every development taking place behind the closed doors of Ookpala's chambers, yet he was taken aback by this address.

"From now on, whenever twins are born, they won't be sacrificed," Ookpala announced to the council's surprise.

"These matters are not discussed in the wee hours of the morning by dragging people out of their beds," Maina protested, trying to change the subject.

"I'm your Oba, and that grants me the authority to call my council at any given time as it suits me. On the other hand, you don't deserve the right to sit and sulk about the choices made by your Oba," Ookpala shot back at Maina.

The council stared in hushed silence. It was clear to see that Ookpala was not going to entertain any arguments.

"There are certain rules that everyone who lives in Benoni will abide by. Killing twins is forbidden from now on, and those who will attempt to take the life of twins will be left to be eaten alive by dogs," Ookpala continued, and the council listened to him in horror.

Maina looked extremely displeased, but he said nothing.

"The practice of bedding virgin priestesses in the coronation ceremony with the intention of breeding an heir will also be forbidden. Those who dare not follow the rule will be burned to death," Ookpala stated. He stared into Maina's eyes, almost challenging him to say something as he laid his agenda in front of the council.

It was not Maina but Esoha who spoke up for the first time during the meeting.

"Forgive me, my Oba. I'm aware that your intentions behind these new rules are pure, and you want nothing but the best for your Obadom," he began. "But Benoni is your homeland, and you know the people. They have been practicing these customs for centuries now, and convincing them otherwise won't be easy."

"I have not finished. Swearing an oath to god Otun by the next Oba in line, from henceforth, must be optional. The next Oba in line must retain the right to choose his own God," Ookpala declared. "Swearing an oath to god Otun is the same as spiritual slavery."

Then he turned to Esoha. "Now, I don't seek to convince people to obey my orders. They are supposed to follow them, or else they will succumb to the horrible consequences."

Esoha bowed in agreement, knowing that Ookpala was serious.

THE HIGH PRIEST GATHERED to caution Oba Ookpala against his decrees that were contrary to god Otun. Oba Ookpala resisted them.

"A declaration will be made tomorrow to issue my orders to cease these vile practices all at once!" Ookpala announced. He thumped the table and left the hall.

His decrees made no difference. Twins were still being killed at birth.

It was a battle. The people of Benoni refused to go to the market for several weeks since more people than usual started birthing twins in the same year. Over time, the decrees of Oba Ookpala eventually won and stayed.

Soon after, people who birthed twins were taken to the Red Palace, where the council heard their cases. The children and their parents were given the opportunity to move to the Old Palace. Here they would be brought up by their parents under the protection of the palace guard.

Thus, the killing of twins finally subsided in Benoni.

WHILE MAINA DID NOT oppose Ookpala's new decrees, at least once a year, he would approach Ookpala with the suggestion to name Omonoma as his legitimate heir, making him the next in line for the throne. Ookpala never paid heed to the pleading and ignored the council, just as he ignored his son.

Sixteen-year-old Omonoma was well aware of his father's refusal to accept him as his heir. However, Maina had told him that he was the rightful heir to the throne and he believed that no one had the right to seize it from him. Omonoma grew up desiring love from his father, who never seemed to care for him.

Omonoma constantly desired his father to acknowledge and validate him. In the absence of a mother and father figure in Omonoma's life, Mishkia, Maina and Esoha had become his mentors. Mishkia was like a mother to Omonoma. They taught him about the politics of the Red Palace while he was also trained to fight.

Ookpala was kept in the dark about Omonoma's training as he had expressed more than once that he didn't want him to have access to any royal traditions taught to the heirs of the Oba. In the sixteen years of Omonoma's life, Oba Ookpala had never even given him permission to visit him.

For the past sixteen years, Omonoma had been playing hide and seek with Ookpala's loyalists. Over the years, he had slowly grown to resent his father for his rejection and dedicated his loyalty to Maina and Esoha.

IT WAS PEDRO'S 16th birthday, and the crew had planned a celebration on the boat to mark the special day. It was believed by the warriors that sixteen was the age when a child finally came of age, so the celebrations were going to be grand.

The celebrations started after dusk. Joaquim and Cleopatra had been busy preparing the meal, especially for Pedro in the kitchen. Pedro was their only child, making him extremely important to them. They loved every moment they could spend with their son since nobody was aware of what tomorrow would hold for the band of warriors.

They lived each day like it was their last. Jimmy had grown older, but his light-hearted nature never changed. Pedro loved his Uncle Jimmy and spent most of the night sitting with him and listening to him narrate tales of his great adventures.

After the grand feast, a rowdy crowd gathered into a circle and picked Pedro up on their shoulders. They swayed to the rhythm of the drums played by Anita as Joaquim and Jimmy emptied the wine glasses.

Cleopatra was content with her life on the African Queen. She had a husband who loved her dearly, a son, and the boat crew, which had turned into her family.

"...... BUT ARE WE EVER GOING to settle on land and stop moving from port to port? Cleopatra asked Joaquim as a loud knock sounded on their bedroom chamber. They were apparently having an argument.

"We have had this discussion so many times" Joaquim sighed. "Okay, my love, you win. We will start looking for a hideout to settle down, so we can stop traveling from port to port."

"Lady Cleo," Jimmy said as he knocked on her chamber's door.

"I'm coming," Cleopatra said. Her voice rang in the chamber shortly before she opened the door. She hid a sharp blade underneath her garment, on her thigh, because they were about to step out.

Cleopatra and Joaquim had become household names as they were lauded for delivering justice to the oppressed. Cleopatra was the brains of the boat. She planned their strategies cleverly and carved a way to win the support of the common men in their battle against the slave traders.

Jimmy had arranged for a meeting with the locals of Aruba Island. They were going to reveal important details and the whereabouts of the slave traders they had been chasing.

Cleopatra was well-trusted when it came to meetings like these. She was a warm person who exuded grace and competence. She knew how to phrase their agenda in a way that was comprehensible to the innocent people of the village.

As Cleopatra and Jimmy got off the boat, Pedro thought it was the perfect time to run to the deck. Pedro was an extremely passionate young man who liked to spend his time training and charming the ladies.

Joaquim was proud of Pedro but also wanted him to focus on familiarizing himself with foreign languages. He wanted Pedro to acquaint himself with the strategies and politics of the slave traders. Pedro was assigned the task of learning a new language every year; this year, it was the Benoni language.

Like any other young pupil, Pedro was more interested in indulging in wild activities. He would sneak off to the deck, where he would practice swordsmanship with his friend, Rico. If they got caught, Uncle Jimmy would often plead for mercy for them from Captain Joaquim.

Although Pedro was only sixteen, he was already a fighter who displayed extraordinary skill, just like Joaquim and Jimmy. He was stealthy, fast, and smart. He could pick the pockets of his victims without them even noticing what was happening.

Before Pedro could brandish his beloved machete at Rico to start a match, Jimmy grabbed his arm from behind, taking Pedro by surprise.

"Here you are, you ruffian. I knew you would use this chance to disobey your father. I couldn't be prouder," Jimmy remarked sarcastically.

Pedro gazed at Jimmy with his big brown eyes. He had attractive facial and physical features. Pedro was as tall as Jimmy and had a muscular physique.

"I apologize, Uncle Jimmy. You are aware of my father. He wouldn't let me practice until I finished my language lesson," Pedro said as he tried to make a failed attempt to justify his disobedience.

"Of course, I understand how difficult and unkind life is for you. I don't know how you put up with the cruelty," Jimmy taunted Pedro again, making him realize that there was no way that Jimmy was going to save him today.

"Will you allow me the honor of walking with you?" Jimmy pleaded sarcastically with a grin on his face. Pedro sighed and nodded.

"So, tell me, Pedro, why were you out here flirting when you are supposed to be completing your lessons?" Jimmy asked. He caught Pedro by surprise, who tried to hide his shock.

"I don't know what you mean," Pedro lied.

"You think I don't know that you risked dodging your tutor to come up to the deck so you could impress Myrcell by brandishing your machete?" Jimmy asked.

He turned in the direction where Myrcell was standing with her friend, giggling.

Pedro had been getting popular as a ladies' man as he surrounded himself with beautiful young women at every opportunity. He would often miss his lessons to meet the girls discreetly, which wasn't as discreet since Jimmy had been aware of his adventures.

EIGHTEEN-YEAR-OLD PEDRO went out gathering food when they docked at Aruba. He heard screams and went to investigate.

He saw a beautiful young girl with curly blond hair. She was screaming for help. There was a large spider tarantula in her hair, and she was going berserk.

Pedro grabbed a stick to pluck out the spider from her hair and as he removed the spider, he accidentally wacked her in the face with it. She screamed.

"Why would you do that? I thought you were trying to help me. Why would you hit me with your stick?" she tossed her hair as Pedro pushed the spider away from her.

"Is that what you will say? I was trying to help you! A thank you would be welcome," Pedro used the opportunity to take a good look at the defiant sixteen-year-old.

"Not bad," he thought. "Hmm, first impression, ha?"

"Yay. I would say thank you if you did not hit me!"

"I am Pedro. What is your name? I think we may have started on the wrong foot," Pedro stretched out his hand.

"I do not introduce myself to strangers, thank you!!" the curly blond-haired girl marched away, leaving his hand stretched out.

Pedro was astounded. He was used to girls fawning over him, but apparently not this heifer.

THE NEXT DAY, AT THE marketplace, Pedro ran into the heifer.

"Hey, you!" he swaggered towards her. "You owe me, and I collect my debts."

"What debt? I don't owe you!" Pedro's heifer responded.

"Yes, you do. I saved you from the spider. Unless you want me to get a spider and put it back in your hair, I suggest you think up a way to pay up." Saying this, he reached into his bag as though he would bring a spider.

"Wait wait wait. Okay, I remember you. What do you want? I do not need a spider in my hair," she gestured with her hands outstretched.

"Your name. What is your name? And say thank you."

Marilla was adventurous.

" My name? If you can catch me, I will tell you my name," so saying, she immediately took off running.

Pedro ran after her. It started raining, and by the time he caught up with her, they were both drenched.

"My name is Marilla," she said as she finally stopped, laughing into his face.

"You are shivering. Come, let us shelter from the rain," Pedro guided Marilla into an underpass beneath a rock.

They spent hours talking and laughing.

PEDRO'S HEART WAS ON a journey of no return on Aruba Island. Their hearts sang songs and danced as their relationship budded with the excitement of first love.

Marilla's family belonged to a peaceful community on their island. They ate vegetables and fruits and didn't hunt animals. They collected aloe herbs after discovering the benefits to one's health. They were unfamiliar with war and fighting. Her family's business was aloe farming.

Pedro asked Marilla to marry him before departing from the island with his crew. When Marilla expressed the desire to marry Pedro, she became the recipient of judgment and backlash from her community. They did not support a marriage between their daughter and a black man. Marilla pleaded with her family to consent to the marriage, but her family was against interracial marriage.

Cleo and Joaquim's exploits were well-known in the places where they had stepped foot. Marilla's family warned her that the African Queen would not rest until it had successfully slayed every slave trader in the sea. They warned Marilla that her fate would not be a happy one and she would become a widow very soon, or her Pedro would be captured as a slave.

"HOW DO I TELL MY PARENTS?" Marilla whispered to Pedro as she snuck out of her house."

"Leave that to me. I am the father, and I am ready to accept my responsibility," Pedro assured Marilla.

When Pedro and Marilla confronted her parents about her pregnancy, Marilla insisted on marrying Pedro.

Her family shunned and ostracized her. They made it very clear to her that she was no longer welcome there. Should she decide to break the marriage and return, she and her interracial child would not be welcome.

Marilla believed that she had found a good man in Pedro. Together, they would overcome the obstacles awaiting them. With this faith in her heart, she decided to leave her community. Pedro took Marilla as his wife, and the crew departed on the African Queen.

When Pedro set sail with Marilla, Marilla had apprehensions about the life they were going to lead. However, her heart was full of love. She was smitten by Pedro and how he treated her. Cleo and Joaquim were also warm and welcomed Marilla with open arms.

However, later, in privacy, Pedro explained to his parents that she had married him on the condition that the couple steers clear of violence.

Joaquim was taken aback by his son's commitment to his wife, but he loved Pedro more than anything else in the world. He agreed to stay away from battles except when they were unavoidable.

Soon, Marilla gave birth to a son. They called him Fredrick. Pedro was a very happy father and Joaquim and Cleopatra were doting grandparents.

True to their word, Joaquim and Cleo steered clear of any skirmishes. The African Queen didn't get involved in any battle for the next few years. Cleopatra was happy pampering her grandson at every opportunity.

Chapter 14: The White Slave

WHEN FREDRICK WAS ALMOST seven years old, slave traders attacked the African Queen. It was the first time that Marilla witnessed a battle. People from the boat's crew were slaughtered in front of her, frightening her to death. After that, she started to realize her family's apprehensions about her future.

Marilla was concerned about the well-being of her son, Fredrick. She became resentful that Pedro and his family lived such a life of violence. Her bitterness started spoiling the relationship between Pedro and Marilla. Marilla longed to see her family again and often spoke about how her life would have been different if she had listened to them and stayed on the island.

One day, Pedro approached Marilla with some news –the African Queen was preparing for a battle against a crew of slave traders. Lemark was one of the biggest slave traders' boats in the ocean and they had been trying to destroy the African Queen for years but in vain.

But the situation was different this time. Lemark had been getting aid from Captain Joaquim's enemies. The boat crews that had been disbanded were united once again, ready to expend all available resources at the prospect of getting revenge.

"I'm aware that our cause is beyond your understanding and you have been against bloodshed, but this time, we can't avoid it, Pedro explained, trying not to alarm Marilla. "We don't know when the attack is going to happen but one thing is for sure, they're out there and they are seeking the opportunity to take us down."

Pedro's and Marilla's marriage had been fraught with fights ever since she'd witnessed the first battle and it was hanging by a thin thread. Marilla had been opposed to the ways of the African Queen and she failed to see the reason behind their quest. All she had wanted was a life devoid of any looming threats but she realized that it wasn't possible as long as she was on the boat.

"I cannot support this foolish decision. But you don't seem to have given much thought to what I want. You will go on to get involved with the bloodshed and won't waste your time considering my reservations," Marilla said angrily.

"This is not just about you and me, Marilla. It's about our people. I cannot allow a massacre to happen in front of my eyes because I want to look after myself and my family only," Pedro argued.

"You will never stop to think about your family, Pedro. The African Queen has always been your weakness. Admit it, you cannot let go of your attachment to battles. I do not want to be a widow, and I do not want you to be captured," Marilla pleaded.

"No one likes to go to battle because it's enjoyable," Pedro stated. "There is a great threat and no one wants to die."

"Except you!" Marilla stated as she glared at Pedro. Then she made up her mind about something. "I have decided to return to my family."

Then, she walked away, with a toss of her long beautiful hair.

After Marilla and Pedro's argument, Marilla did not leave her chamber all day and she asked people to give her the liberty of spending some time alone with herself. Pedro respected Marilla's wishes and decided not to interfere with her.

AT TWO HOURS PAST MIDNIGHT, Marilla heard a loud thud on her door. She opened the door to see if there was someone outside. She walked out into the hall, but she couldn't find anyone. Then, Marilla heard a scream coming from the hallway beside her chamber. She ran to see what was happening but when she reached there, someone grabbed her and stuffed a piece of cloth in her mouth.

She struggled to escape from the person holding her but couldn't manage to do so. As she tried to escape, she felt a hard, sharp object hit her on the head and she lost consciousness.

After what seemed like ages, Marilla woke up to the sight of a woman applying ointment to her injury.

"What is happening?" Marilla asked. She suddenly realized that she was not on the African Queen anymore.

"You will figure it out," the woman answered coldly.

"I need to go...get to the party. It's my son's seventh birthday today," mumbled Marilla.

Marilla looked around the place and found that she was surrounded by people in ragged clothes lying on the floor. Some were feeding children food that appeared like mashed rice and some were fiddling with the chains tied to their feet.

"Get up!" the woman ordered Marilla, loudly. "Still talking about a birthday party!! Rubbish!"

Marilla struggled to stand up on her feet. She looked down and found that she was also tied to chains. The woman gave a jerk to Marilla's chain so she stood upright.

'Oh my! What are these?' Marilla pondered.

FREDRICK WAS TURNING seven. The African Queen's crew members were occupied with the preparations for Frederick's birthday party. Jimmy and Anita wanted to make the night memorable as they anticipated the battle between the African Queen and Lemark would start soon. Marilla was not present as she had locked herself in her chamber. They decided to carry on without disturbing her, per her wish.

The ceremony to celebrate his birthday went on till the early hours of the morning. Realizing that Marilla was still absent, Pedro started to look for her. When Pedro went to their chambers to fetch Marilla, he was surprised to see it was empty. He couldn't find her.

Frantically, Pedro searched everywhere. The crew questioned everyone about her whereabouts. Pedro went to Jimmy, and when he found him, he was hanging his head low.

"Where is she?" Pedro asked. He could sense what was coming. He expected the worst. She had threatened to leave him already.

"No one knows. A young girl on the crew saw her carrying a bag of clothes," Jimmy said sadly as he broke the news to him. Pedro remembered how she'd said she was going back to her family. Apparently, Marilla had made good on her threat and left the African Queen. He was devastated by Marilla's departure.

SOON, MARILLA WAS TRANSPORTED to a different place where the owner of a plantation called the Jackerville had been awaiting her arrival. The word had been spread that a woman had been captured from the African Queen by the slave traders of Lemark. The woman was not only extremely beautiful, she also had a regal bearing.

"One would think she is the African Queen herself!! Hahaha, but she is white," the woman who'd been tending to Marilla's injury said to the plantation owner.

"Look at you, so enchanting," the old plantation owner remarked when he saw Marilla.

"Why have I been brought here? Don't you know who I am?" Marilla screamed.

"Yes, I do, and that's exactly why you're here. See, you have been captured by your husband's enemy, and it's not going to be easy for you unless-"

"Unless our owner, Borsan, changes his mind considering how enchanting his new slave appears," the man standing beside Borsan completed his sentence.

Borsan grinned. Marilla stood there frozen; her fate was decided by her captors. She had no way of escaping as she was unfamiliar with the people around there.

NO ONE KNEW OF MARILLA'S whereabouts. Pedro went back to Marilla's home, but they told him she was not there, and the family told him that Marilla and him were not welcome.

"She probably left you but was too ashamed to show her face back here!" they said.

Pedro was hurt by her departure, but he decided to act otherwise in public for the benefit of his son. He was shattered that Marilla would choose to abandon not only him but her son too.

"Pedro, any woman who can walk away from her child is not worth your time," Joaquim consoled him.

"I will take care of Fredrick. Forget Marilla. If she doesn't want to be with you, and has chosen to hide from you. Forget her!" Cleopatra roared.

Chapter 15: A Son Returns

IT HAD BEEN TEN YEARS since Marilla left the African Queen without a trace. Borsan had made sure that Marilla was wedded to him, then she was forced to live a life among the slaves!

Marilla often wondered if she had been talking to Pedro on a different day, would her life have turned out so differently? She had been forced to marry her captor and was sentenced to a life of a glorified slave. Marilla's kindness drew the people on the plantation toward her. Marilla managed to befriend some of the slaves and tried to find a way to send word to the husband she chose for herself, Pedro.

Marilla's attempts at finding someone who could reach out to Pedro on her behalf had proved to be unfruitful. She had to be discreet with her plan since Borsan would kill her if he discovered that his prized possession, his trophy slave wife, was trying to go back to her family.

After all these years, Marilla had come to the sad conclusion that Pedro had forgotten her, deciding to let her go since they were constantly fighting. She wondered if Pedro would have come for her if she had been captured on a different day. She braved her fate and became the best wife she could be to Borsan.

Borsan had become kind to Marilla as the years went by. He treated her better and she lived the life as a Madam of the plantation.

THE VOICES TORMENTED Ookpala as he grew older. He was in his sixties and almost driven mad owing to the chaos the voices had created for him. Efe had been by Ookpala's side for decades. He refused to give up on his Oba as his faith remained strong in the face of challenges.

"Efe! Efe!" Ookpala yelled.

"I'm here, my Oba," Efe said. He was sitting in a seat in Ookpala's chamber when the latter got startled.

"I need to repent for my sins," Ookpala stated as he got up from his bed.

"Oba, you need to rest," Efe replied as he tried to calm Ookpala, who didn't appear to be in his senses.

"I said I need to repent!" Ookpala yelled again. "I had a dream. In my dream, I was told to pray. To repent and all will be well. I have not been able to pray to my one true God all these years. I thought he had forgotten me and abandoned me!"

Tears streamed down his face as he sobbed.

"In my dream, He told me that He will never leave or forsake me. He told me that He is faithful and willing to forgive me. All I need to do is pray," Ookpala continued through his tears.

"Call upon Him for help, and He will answer me.

"Efe, I have been so ashamed all these years. I have been so embarrassed, and my voice had been locked up inside me. I thought he will reject me, the same way I had rejected him. But he said No. He came to me."

Ookpala continued sobbing.

"He told me that all I need to do is believe in my heart and confess him with my mouth, and no matter the sin I have committed, I will be saved."

Ookpala tried to leave his bedchamber, but Efe held him back. It was not the first time Ookpala had become so agitated or tried going out in a disarrayed state. Once, Ookpala left his bedchamber in the middle of the night, and when the palace guards found him the next day, he told them that he was looking for his family.

"You need to stay steady," Efe told Ookpala, who was resisting him.

Ookpala dropped to his knees and bowed his head. Then, tears flowed from his eyes, and he started mumbling words that Efe could barely make out.

"Oh God, forgive me for breaking the edge. Forgive me for my sins. Forgive me for disobeying you and renouncing my faith. I have been ashamed and thought I could hide from you. I felt so guilty that the words to repent were locked up inside me. I am in chains. I see myself in chains every time I close my eyes to sleep.

"Please God, forgive me. I repent of my sin. I ask you to forgive me. I believe that Jesus is the son of God. He arose from the dead and He is alive forevermore.

"I renounce my blood ties with the god Otun. I ask for your help. Liberate me from the bondage of god Otun.

"I accept Jesus as my Lord and Savior. I ask that you restore my faith in you. I beg you to return my family to me. I beg you for your forgiveness, in the name of Jesus Christ, I pray," Ookpala bowed his head as he knelt to God.

On realizing what was happening, Efe stopped holding Ookpala.

THAT VERY NIGHT OOKPALA had another dream. The Coronation Ground was soaked with blood, and he was held in chains at god Otun's idol shrine. The god Otun's idol was his warden with his axe and whip.

Ookpala saw the image of a man from the sky that appeared like light. The light enveloped Ookpala. Where he had previously felt very weak, as the man gave him a cup to drink from, Ookpala felt strengthened. In his state, with the power transferred to him from the light, Ookpala exerted himself lightly and the chains broke apart.

He then struck the god Otun idol that had chained him all his life and smashed it to pieces. Ookpala heard a still, small voice. It spoke in a whisper that sounded like thunder.

"Ookpala! You are free!"

He was told to walk out of the shrine. And as he limped out of the shrine, he opened his eyes, he realized he was dreaming, but his prayers had been answered.

" Will I hear the voices again?" Ookpala thought to himself.

He stayed awake during the night, afraid he would hear the voices again, but he did not hear them.

The next morning, Ookpala noticed that for the first time in years he had slept peacefully that night without the voices or tossing.

"Efe, I am free. The voices are gone. Listen let me tell you about my dream last night, before my peaceful sleep...."

Efe on witnessing the peaceful sleep of Ookpala and hearing about Ookpala's dream, gave his life to Christ the next morning.

Ookpala started telling everyone about Jesus and how he had rescued him from god Otun. He told the entire Kingdom, "Henceforth, there will be freedom of worship. Anyone wishing to convert from god Otun to the one true God whose son is Jesus should believe and confess with their mouths."

As the Obadom witnessed Ookpala's recovery, and heard Ookpala's message, lots of people converted to Christianity. The people became hopeful for the restoration of Benoni, which had been left unattended since Ookpala started hearing voices.

The people dared to hope that the days of a bloody Benoni were over. A new and glorious Benoni was born under the rulership of Oba Ookpala.

Chapter 16: Counterfeit Confession

"MY OBA, SOMEONE REQUESTS for an audience with you, but she demands discretion," Efe told Ookpala, who was writing a letter in his bedchamber.

"Bring her along," Ookpala told Efe.

A faint shadow of a lean woman appeared at the doorsteps of a chamber. She was short and wore a green tunic. The woman looked frightened as she entered the bedchamber.

"My Oba, I bear information that might bring harm upon me if the word ever gets out."

"What is your name?" Ookpala asked.

"Semar. I have been serving the Obadom since I was ten."

"And what kind of information might this be?"

"I'm aware of what happened to your family," Semar said hesitantly.

Ookpala looked at Efe, who seemed as astounded as him. Ookpala had been searching for his family for decades in vain, yet he had still not given up all hope. Even now, he was desperate to find out anything about what happened to his family.

"Continue," Ookpala commanded her, setting aside the letter.

"I witnessed your children and wife getting slain. Their slaughter was plotted as soon as they arrived here. You were occupied with the coronation ceremony when your sons were poisoned, and your wife was killed."

Ookpala felt the world around him collapse. He was too numb to process what was happening. He held the edge of his seat to stand and stay steady as he stared into the eyes of Semar.

"Where were you when I was going mad searching for my family?" Ookpala asked incredulously.

"I was threatened by the council to not reveal anything to you. They threatened all the witnesses to stay silent, and if we didn't, they would have killed us along with our families," Semar explained.

"Why now? Why do you come forward now?" Ookpala asked, still finding it hard to believe.

"I am sick, my Oba. I am dying and do not wish to leave this world without relieving you of the mystery surrounding the disappearance of your family. But I am still afraid. I wish to be discreet and stay anonymous."

Ookpala promised Semar discretion about the matter. Efe was given the responsibility of ensuring Semar's family's safety.

With a heavy heart, Ookpala ordered a private funeral to be arranged for his late wife and sons. He wanted the funeral to be held away from the Red Palace so no one could find out about what he had learned.

"I WILL AVENGE THE INJUSTICE that was brought upon you. Your deaths will be avenged," Ookpala swore to the graves of his family.

He stood there watching everything quietly. When Efe came to stand beside him, he sighed heavily.

"I cannot trust anyone except you, Efe," Ookpala said during the funeral. "My suspicions have become true. They have kept me in the dark for many years. My entire family was stolen from me and slain while I was held prisoner by those so-called priests in the name of a coronation ceremony."

"I mourn their loss with you," Efe promised.

"As I was getting crowned, my children and wife were getting killed! Their memories have tormented me. I have spent so many years wondering where they were, not even knowing that they have been long dead."

Ookpala's eyes had turned red, and the vein in his forehead was thumping so hard, it seemed like it would burst.

"I will crush the council that sentenced my family to death. I will have their souls ripped apart in front of each other. Maina and Esoha will reap what they sowed," Ookpala vowed as he stared into Efe's eyes.

Efe had known Ookpala long enough to understand that he had had enough. Ookpala meant what he said. He was not going to spare anyone for the sins they had committed.

"I might have grown old, but I will stand by your side and for your cause till my last breath, my Oba," Efe vowed to Ookpala.

Chapter 17: The Darkest Hour

"FATHER, HELP ME," OOKPALA prayed. "I have long done things according to my own wishes, but no more. Please guide me. Let me do what only you will get the glory from. Teach me how to deal with my enemies. In Jesus' name, Amen."

The very next morning, the entire population of Benoni was summoned to the Red Palace. Everyone had to be present on the grounds to witness the address of Oba Ookpala.

"I stand before you to be the bearer of bad news. The Obadom has been betrayed by the people who were supposed to serve it. Your Queen Iredia was slain along with my twin sons in the halls of the Old Palace," Ookpala declared.

The entire audience in attendance went silent. The people of Benoni had been volunteering to find the whereabouts of Queen Iredia and her sons for decades now. Groups of ten had been rotating the search for years. People were still journeying and trying to find signs of the lost Queen of Benoni and her children.

"The people who killed your Queen and my children were none other than those who sit on the council. Every person involved in the slaughter of Queen Iredia and the throne's heirs will soon witness the justice of the Obadom. They shall be executed right before your eyes to serve a lesson for their generations to come," Ookpala stated as he finished his address.

Efe gave Ookpala the names of people involved in the slaughter of Queen Iredia and his sons. Maina and Esoha were declared the primary culprits of the massacre. Their trial was scheduled to happen in front of the entire population of Benoni.

Ookpala ordered the culprits to be imprisoned until their trial date. After this was done, he called for a council meeting. He was waiting for Efe to arrive at the council meeting when Ebere, Mishkia's alleged nephew came running into the hall.

"Oba!" he yelled.

"What is happening? Who allowed you to come here?" Efe yelled as he appeared.

"Don't you remember me? I am Mishkia's nephew. I need to speak to the Oba," Ebere tried to explain. "It is a matter of great importance!"

"You can't just barge into the Oba's presence whenever you like. Take this man away," Efe instructed the guards.

Ebere was dragged out of the hall and taken into the court, where Mishkia tried to stop the guards.

"He is of my house! Leave him!" Mishkia yelled furiously.

"I'm afraid we can't do that. We have orders," one of the guards said.

The guards dragged Ebere out of the courtyard as Mishkia kept screaming. They didn't listen to her once. She was helpless as Efe was nowhere to be found as well.

THAT NIGHT, TWO HOURS before sunrise, Ookpala's bedchamber was invaded by an army of men dressed in black. They were carrying machetes, and one of the men held a dagger at Ookpala's throat.

"You will regret doing this!" Ookpala warned them as he shot his bloody stare at the man holding the dagger.

"And who will make us regret it? Your son will become an Oba soon, and you will rot in prison," the men threatened.

Ookpala was thrown inside the dungeon of the Red Palace. He was forced to stay there without any access to food or water for days. The dungeon was dark and swarmed with bugs. Ookpala didn't ask the guards for food even once, no matter how difficult survival became inside the dungeon. Instead, Ookpala fed on the roaches in his cell.

"My Oba," Maina called out in a mocking voice to Ookpala while standing outside his cell. "We have a proposition for you since you have served the Obadom with all your heart."

Maina's tone was more sarcastic than convincing. Ookpala faced the wall of his dungeon. He didn't wish to look at Maina, who had betrayed him and put him in the dungeon.

"You can either renounce your throne for your rightful heir, Omonoma, or name him heir so he will be able to rule in your place. If you accept any of these conditions, your life shall be spared, and Efe will also be released," Maina told him.

"You shouldn't waste your time here. I will never agree to your terms," Ookpala finally answered.

"You might want to consider if you wish to live," Maina said.

"I would rather die," Ookpala said sternly.

MAINA LEFT THE DUNGEON and went to the Old Palace, where Esoha was waiting for him. Omonoma was also seated right beside Esoha and discussing a matter that seemed to be of great importance.

"He refused," Maina informed them.

"As we expected. Omonoma will still be crowned as the next Oba tomorrow, according to our plan," Esoha got up from his seat.

"We will require the people's support if we crown him," Maina said.

"I'm the rightful heir to the throne. We don't need anyone's support. Their heads will bow down once I unleash the machete," Omonoma boasted.

A BLOODY CORONATION ceremony was held where Omonoma was crowned as the next Oba of Benoni. He left the Priest Ground after seven days disregarding that the barbaric tradition of the coronation and the breeding of the reserve heirs, along with the seven-day seclusion post-coronation, had been abolished by Oba Ookpala. They used it to their advantage to revert to the traditions of the old.

Omonoma immediately summoned all council members and declared the execution of Ebere to be done immediately for daring to attempt a betrayal of their coup and plot.

Maina fought against Ebere's execution, but Omonoma refused to listen to reason.

"I need to speak to you privately," Maina entreated Omonoma.

"I don't have the time right now. We will speak later," Omonoma responded.

Ebere was imprisoned in the dungeon next to Ookpala's for some hours. Ookpala had been barely eating as the torture he endured became more brutal with each passing day.

"You came for me that day," Ookpala spoke to Ebere for the first time.

"I did," Ebere said.

"What was it about?"

"The coup. Esoha, Maina, and Omonoma had plotted against you and planned to usurp your rule. I'm Mishkia's son from her teenage indiscretion. Chief Maina is my stepfather. He is unaware. He believes I am a nephew to his wife. Omonoma is my adopted half-brother! He is unaware, but he is not your son."

"How is that possible?" Ookpala asked, stunned.

"He was foisted on you by my stepfather years ago to usurp the throne. Chief Maina swapped your child with his and Mishkia's adopted son after having a stillbirth when my mother was his wet nurse.

They found out that I was about to reveal their plot, and I was captured as a traitor," Ebere explained, with his head hanging down.

Oba Ookpala was speechless.

Before Ookpala could respond, Ebere was relocated into an isolated dungeon. The very next day, without allowing Ebere to speak, lest he spill any more details, he was removed and executed privately by Omonoma.

Mishkia was unaware of the happenings. When she found out, it was too late. She swore vengeance upon Maina, who had insisted on foisting Omonoma on Oba Ookpala.

Now, her beloved first son had breathed his last! Killed by his brother!

She cried quietly as she reflected on what she had done. It felt like she was being punished for having done the wrong things.

She decided to make things right.

"MY OBA," A VOICE ECHOED behind the rails of Ookpala's dungeon.

"Who is it?"

"It is Omo, my Oba."

Omo was one of Ookpala's aides in the palace. He had been serving in the Red Palace since he was six years old.

"I have brought a message from Madam Mishkia."

"I don't want to hear it!" Oba Ookpala screamed. "I cannot trust her anymore."

"Oba, Madam Mishkia has sent for help from the African Queen," Omo stated. "Please hold your peace."

"Excuse me?" Ookpala answered. "What does that have to do with me?"

"We shall have a savior soon from the African Queen. You need to hold steady and keep your faith intact during this challenging time," Omo entreated.

"Why would someone from the African Queen help me?"

"They are a private military who owe Mishkia some favors," whispered Omo.

"Hmm," Ookpala responded.

OMO STARTED REGULARLY coming to see Ookpala. He was the same age as Omonoma. His parents were believed to have died when Omo was born. Maina brought him to the Old Palace when he was six years old, and he had served at the palace since then.

The bond between Omo and Ookpala strengthened over the months he spent in the dungeon. Omo ensured that Ookpala didn't lose his faith in life. He encouraged him to eat, read and play board games with him. He had become his sole support during the reign of the cruel Oba Omonoma.

Omonoma continued to rule Benoni and held the Obadom under his reign devoid of mercy. He stopped meeting with the council chiefs and started making his own decisions. People who dared disagree with Omonoma were rewarded with imprisonment and were never seen again.

There was no one to question Omonoma's reign of terror.

Maina remained his right hand, and Esoha, his Chief Palace Guard but it was clear that he owed them no loyalty. He was also merciless toward the ones he felt had wronged him. He would often have Efe beaten with whips when a conflict occurred. Omonoma didn't believe in mercy, just like his father, Maina. Fear was the only tool for keeping Omonoma's Obadom in place.

Chapter 18: Mirror Image

"ADETOLA WILL BE HERE shortly. One of our sailors has spotted his boat scouting around Saba Island. So we should be expecting him and his wife in an hour or two," Anita informed Cleo, who had been talking with Jimmy.

"Someone should be there to receive them," Jimmy suggested while staring at the map lying in front of him on a round table.

"Perhaps, Fredrick should be the one to greet them. It's time he starts stepping up for our affairs," Cleo spoke in a subtle tone, hinting at uncertainty.

"I don't know if Fredrick will agree-"

"It's not up to him to agree or not. He is seventeen. When Pedro was his age, he had already picked up the machete against the enemy, yet here he is, bickering about the injustice in his life as if he is the first one to endure all the misgivings of life..."

A TALL FIGURE DESCENDED on the boat right in front of Frederick. He tossed his cloak at one of the people walking behind him and marched towards Frederick.

"Greetings," Fredrick exclaimed as the tall man approached him.

"And you must be?"

"I'm Pedro's son, Fredrick."

"Greetings! Fredrick. I'm Adetola, I am the weapon supplier. I have heard about you from your father," he said as he firmly shook Fredrick's lean hand. "This is my wife, Oghale."

Fredrick walked Adetola, Oghale, and his crew to the stone house where Cleo and Joaquim were staying on Saba Island. Joaquim had finally succumbed to Cleopatra's pressure and settled on the land, building them a stone house.

Oghale kept eyeing Fredrick as if she was trying to figure out something. Joaquim welcomed Adetola and Oghale once they were inside the house.

"Quite a place you have made for yourself," Adetola commented.

"Well, it only took us many years," Joaquim remarked.

"It must have been a tough task to keep this base's whereabouts undisclosed from everyone."

"It used to be a part of Saba Island. Since it is remote, nobody paid any attention to it, so we thought it would be best to build our base here," Joaquim explained.

"What about your spy network?"

"We have established a reputation for our spies. They roam around the streets and have built strong connections. People who have lost their loved ones to the slave trade know where to find our people," Cleo interrupted the conversation between Joaquim and Adetola.

"Iredia?" Adetola's wife, Oghale, exclaimed when she saw Cleopatra.

"I'm Cleopatra, wife of Captain Joaquim."

"What? Are you not Princess Iredia? Your grandson is the spitting image of Prince Ookpala of Benoni Kingdom," Oghale insisted.

"How so?" Cleo wondered. "You must have me confused."

"Oghale, how are you doing?" interrupted Joaquim. "Please come with me. I have some wares that most certainly will interest you." He pulled Oghale away from completing her conversation with Cleopatra.

"Whoa! What a strange world. I used to know a prince, and your grandson is his spitting image. Only your grandson is more white than black. Even your wife, but for the fact that she told me I am confused, I would swear I birthed her twins!"

"Interesting!!" mused Joaquim. "She is my wife, we do not have twins, and I would appreciate it if you do not bring up such matters anymore when speaking with her."

Oghale, the midwife who birthed Cleopatra's twins when she was with Prince Ookpala as Iredia, immediately backed up and apologized for overstepping.

Cleopatra recalling that she was raped before getting pregnant with Pedro, wondered if she had been raped by the so-called prince Ookpala of Benoni kingdom.

Before she could enquire further, Joaquim and Oghale had left her side. She decided not to broach the subject to allow history to sleep undisturbed.

MARILLA STILL COULDN'T get the word out to Pedro. She remained hopeful that one day she would be reunited with Pedro, but again and again, she was thwarted – her release from her prison was nowhere near.

Pedro, on the other hand, was unaware of Marilla's abduction. He believed that Marilla had left of her own accord, unable to come to terms with the bloody path the African Queen wanted to take.

Little did he know that his wife had been trying to reunite with him for years in vain.

Chapter 19: The Debt

THE AFRICAN QUEEN HAD witnessed challenging times and peaked in its glory, yet it was time for the boat to enter a new era. Cleo had made it her goal to help her son Pedro understand the implications and what it meant once he took over the African Queen.

After Cleo and Joaquim were satisfied that the African Queen was in safe hands, they resorted to a life of retirement. The couple was in their sixties and were grandparents to Fredrick as well. They wanted to live a life unaccompanied by battles and mercenaries.

It was finally time for Pedro to take his oath for the African Queen.

"I swear to fight the injustice brought upon common people by slave traders. I shall not rest until every slave trader meets his grave fate of succumbing to the very chains in which they hold others hostage. I will protect my crew with my life and will never fall short of my duties," Pedro swore in front of the entire crew on the deck of the African Queen.

Joaquim handed Pedro the precious dagger he had been carrying for decades. The dagger cemented Pedro's rank as the commander of the African Queen and its mercenaries. Cleo gazed at Pedro with utmost affection as he took the dagger from his father.

"Commander of the mercenaries! Commander of the African Queen!" Joaquim announced as he pulled Pedro's arm in the air.

"Hear, hear!" the crew cheered. They rose and roared with enthusiasm as they witnessed their new commander ascending the ranks. They shook hands with Pedro and embraced him as the sound of drumming took over.

"AGAIN," JIMMY TOLD Fredrick.

Fredrick swung his machete and pointed it at Jimmy's throat but Jimmy dodged by hitting the pointer of Fredrick's machete. Jimmy thought he had finally managed to lead in the fight and smiled, but Fredrick took advantage of the moment and hit Jimmy's machete so hard that it swung out of his hand.

"Admit it, you're rusty now," Fredrick smirked.

"No, you're just younger," Jimmy growled.

Fredrick was eighteen years old and had grown into a fine machetes man. He also participated in training for the possible battles and had aced the practice. Jimmy was proud of Fredrick and how far he had come since his mother's disappearance.

"I need to leave now," Fredrick excused himself after the fight.

Fredrick started to climb downstairs, but when he reached the bottom, he heard the familiar voice of his "uncle" Rico, Pedro's best friend and second-in-command.

"Wasn't that hard to catch you since you stand out," Rico teased Fredrick.

"Enough with this," Fredrick said as he tried to get rid of Rico, but he seemed to be in a mood to taunt Fredrick further.

"Or what? You would have our commander, your father, string me up?" Rico teased again.

Fredrick was angry, but this wasn't the time to pick a fight with Rico. Over time, he had become used to the constant taunts since he was the fairest-skinned person on the crew.

It was common for people in the crew and their children to pick on Fredrick due to his skin color. He had grown a thick skin to escape the taunts and no longer cared about what people said about his interracial appearance.

ANOTHER EPISODE OF lightning struck a dense tree, and it fell to the ground, catching fire. A woman hung on to the branch of a thick tree, trying to survive through the night. She was drenched in water and continued shivering as the rain got wilder and louder.

Two children were lying on the ground, covered by leaves. Their faces were blurred and their eyes were closed. They appeared to be dead, but their bodies had been abandoned on the ground as if they never belonged to anyone.

"Aaaaaa!" the woman screamed as she felt a sharp sting in her foot.

When the woman tried to see what caused the sting, she found a snake staring into her face. She realized that the snake had bitten her, and the venom was starting to spread in her body.

The snake stared at the woman as she started to lose her balance, no longer able to cling to the branch that had been supporting her all this while. Her head started spinning, and she let go of the branch, falling to the ground.

BAMMM!!

"Noooo!" Cleo screamed as she woke up. For some strange reason, her recurring nightmares were getting more frequent since Adetola and Oghale's visit.

"It was just a dream. You're okay," Joaquim soothed her. He held Cleo in his arms, who was sweating profusely.

"It seemed so real. It was more real than ever before. I think these nightmares are trying to tell me something," Cleo said, panting.

" Oghale, Captain Adetola's wife, mentioned to me that she birthed my twins. I keep dreaming of twins. It is just so confusing." Cleopatra shook her head, trying to clear it of any remaining fog.

Joaquim remained quiet.

It was becoming harder for him to conceal the truth from her. He harbored guilt, but he also treasured Cleo more than anything. He couldn't risk losing her, so he chose to remain silent.

THE AFRICAN QUEEN DOCKED at an island near Benoni to get the supplies it needed for the journey ahead. Pedro was busy discussing strategies with Jimmy when Rico came running.

"Someone from Benoni wants to deliver a message," Rico said.

"Benoni?" Pedro asked.

He was clueless about the affairs of Benoni, but he was intrigued as he had been made to learn the Benoni language at a young age. Joaquim had never talked about the affairs of Benoni to him.

Jimmy was immediately alarmed when he heard the name of Benoni. He wasn't aware of the current turn of events in the Kingdom, but he knew that Benoni had a long-lived association with Captain Joaquim.

"Send the person here," Jimmy told Rico.

Pedro looked at Jimmy with questioning eyes. Jimmy seemed uneasy, and Pedro had never seen him appear this disturbed.

A thin man draped in black walked over to Jimmy and Pedro. He was carrying a parchment in his hand that was folded.

"Which one of you is Captain Joaquim?" the man asked.

"What's the message?" Jimmy asked.

"This message needs to be delivered to Captain Joaquim of the African Queen."

"It will be passed on to him. I'm his son and commander of this boat," Pedro said.

The man pondered for a few moments but then decided to hand it over to Pedro. He left the boat immediately after giving the parchment to Pedro.

"Omonoma, the wrongful Oba of Benoni, has executed Ebere, Mishkia's son. The debt must be paid and the payment shall be the restoration of the crown that will allow Oba Ookpala to return to his throne," Pedro read out the message.

Pedro didn't wait for Jimmy to respond and walked straight to his father's chamber. He wanted answers.

"What kind of debt is this, and why are the happenings of the Kingdom of Benoni of concern to us?" Pedro asked Joaquim, who stared at the message in disbelief.

Joaquim didn't know how to protect Pedro from the truth he had been hiding for a long time. So he tried to avoid the subject by making up excuses.

"It shouldn't concern you," Joaquim told Pedro.

"We can't have anything to do with these kingdoms and their internal politics. It's their conflict, not ours. They were never our allies and never will be. What we need to do is focus on our mission," Pedro explained to Joaquim.

Joaquim, aware that he had a debt to pay to Mishkia, found himself feeling conflicted. He didn't want Pedro to find out the truth no matter what. However, sending Pedro to Benoni would mean that he was going to discover the secret that had been hidden from him at some point.

"I'm going to decline the request. We are at a critical stage of the mission, and we will need all our mercenaries. No, I don't think we can afford any distractions," Pedro explained.

Joaquim nodded but didn't say anything.

"What are you two talking about here?" Cleo asked as she emerged from the chamber.

Cleo saw the parchment in Joaquim's hand and tried to reach for it, but Joaquim tried to keep it away from her.

"What is it?" Cleo asked.

"It's sorted," Joaquim answered, trying to change the subject.

Cleo snatched the parchment from Joaquim's hand and began reading the message. Joaquim stared at her anxiously, hoping that she wouldn't be able to recall anything by the mention of Benoni.

"What is this debt, and why don't I know about this matter?" Cleo asked in a puzzled tone.

"I have encountered several instances in the past where I came across kingdoms that needed my assistance so I could also get something in return. However, this was when the African Queen was not the sole purpose of my life, so I never considered it important to discuss," Joaquim lied as he tried to make up a scenario.

"You're hiding something, Joaquim," Cleo remarked.

Joaquim tried to avoid eye contact with Cleo, who kept staring at him. He knew it was hard for him to lie when Cleo looked at him. She had a way of staring into people's souls that could weaken them, especially Joaquim.

"The concern here is that Pedro will be departing soon for the mission, and without him, we wouldn't be able to help any kingdom. This is the worst time to request help. I'm afraid we'll have to make the crucial decision of turning the plea down," Cleo reasoned.

"I agree, Mother. The mission should be our sole focus for now, not some Oba in the Benoni Kingdom," Pedro reaffirmed.

Pedro left to attend to his other affairs. Before Joaquim could leave, Cleo grabbed his hand. Joaquim knew what was coming but hoped the situation could be avoided.

"You're going to explain to me what the debt is all about," Cleo stated. She stared at Joaquim, determined to find out the truth.

"The matter belongs in the past, and it must stay there," Joaquim replied as he tried to put an end to the subject, but it only made Cleo more curious.

"This is the first time you're holding back. You cannot have any secrets from me. We have spent a lifetime together," Cleo insisted. She tried to make Joaquim listen to her.

Joaquim couldn't defend himself anymore. He decided to tell her the truth.

"You're aware of my deceased wife, Lushinna, and her terrible fate, right?"

Cleo nodded.

"The debt I owe is to her sister, named Mishkia, who rescued me on that terrible day. It brings back tragic memories, and that's why I didn't want to indulge in the subject."

Cleo was aware of his tragic past and how it affected Joaquim in the most terrible way. She knew she had to stop right there and leave the subject alone.

"I feel guilty that I made you revisit a terrible time," Cleo said.

Joaquim looked at Cleo's face. She trusted him, and he felt terrible for letting her down. As he struggled with the words to use in his confession, Fredrick walked in and interrupted the moment.

"I will tell her later. After the mission. She may understand better after visiting her lost kingdom." Joaquim promised himself.

Chapter 20: The Mission

THE FOLLOWING NIGHTS Joaquim spent were restless and sleepless. He felt an ache in his heart caused by the refusal of the African Queen to help Mishkia.

Joaquim felt like he was being tested, and he thought that he was failing. He didn't want to lose Cleo, but he also couldn't let Mishkia down. After all, he owed his life to her.

It was four past midnight when Joaquim was woken up by the clanking of machetes. Pedro was about to depart for his mission. Joaquim got out of his bed and ran towards the dock.

"Pedro, wait," Joaquim said, panting.

Mercenaries were being loaded in the smaller boats floating around their sailing boat. Pedro was stuffing his jacket with daggers and knives. He turned around to find Joaquim looking like he had run a mile.

"We cannot wait. Get on the boat, everyone!" Rico shouted.

Pedro ran toward Joaquim and embraced him before hopping into one of the boats carrying the mission crew.

It was too late. Joaquim had lost the chance to talk to Pedro. He had made up his mind to speak with Pedro about answering the cry for help from Benoni. But, perhaps, a part of Joaquim didn't want the conversation to happen in the first place.

Tired and disappointed in himself, Joaquim returned to his chamber. He spent the rest of the time staring at the ceiling, contemplating the turn of events. The thought of Mishkia's suffering kept haunting him. She didn't deserve his silence, but he was helpless.

Joaquim started deeming himself a selfish man who couldn't repay the debt owed to someone who had given him back his life. If it weren't for Mishkia, he would never have made it out alive after the slave traders were finished destroying his first boat, the Portugal Queen.

Again, Mishkia gave him another chance at life when she brought Cleo to him. He would have never loved again or had a family if Cleo had never arrived. Mishkia was the reason Joaquim had a life filled with love.

Joaquim kept thinking about how he could help Mishkia, but nothing made sense to him. The choice between helping Mishkia and the risk of losing Cleo was driving him insane.

After a few hours, Joaquim decided to talk to Jimmy. He was one of the few people who was aware of his past with Mishkia. Perhaps, he could help counsel him on the matter.

Before Joaquim could walk to Jimmy's chamber, he saw him approaching his chamber while he was standing at the door. Jimmy looked furious. His lips were pursed and his hands folded behind his back.

"This way," Jimmy stated as he guided Joaquim to the dark pathway behind the chamber.

Joaquim followed him.

"Did you tell him?" Jimmy asked.

"There wasn't enough time-"

"Not enough time to tell him that his father needs him? That he might be in grave danger?" Jimmy asked furiously. "He is the heir to that throne! His royal blood is enough reason for him to be extra careful out there." Jimmy's fists were clenched as the veins in his neck protruded with his galloping pulse.

"You are well aware of the implications of this affair, Jimmy."

"How could you let him leave without telling him the truth? What if he never returns? What if he dies without knowing his royal heritage? He was not in danger anymore, but with this complication arising, he should know," Jimmy thundered. He attacked Joaquim with his questions.

"I am his father," Joaquim looked around to ensure no one was within earshot.

"You know what I mean," Jimmy whispered.

"I can't lose my family," Joaquim said with pleading eyes.

"You're making a grave mistake. You cannot keep a son from his aging father, who needs him to regain his throne!! If you don't reveal the truth, then I will," Jimmy threatened.

Joaquim watched Jimmy walk away from him with fists clenched. He knew he had to make a choice now, or he would never be able to live in peace. Apparently, the tenure of his borrowed happiness was coming to an end.

"WHAT IS THE MATTER?" Fredrick asked Cleo as they climbed down the stairs to meet Joaquim.

"I'm as clueless as you," Cleo told her grandson.

They reached the bottom of the stairs and looked across the room. Joaquim was standing in the corner, lost in thought.

"Joaquim?" Cleo said.

Joaquim turned and walked towards his wife and grandson.

"I have decided on a matter that has been haunting me for a while. I hope to have your support in my decision," Joaquim said.

"What decision?"

"We need to answer Benoni's cry for help."

"We have talked about it before-"

"I owe my life to Mishkia. What kind of man will I be remembered as if I abandoned someone who rescued me?" Joaquim asked. His voice sounded more determined than ever.

"What about our force? Pedro left with a large part of our mercenaries. If we're going to rescue someone in a kingdom, then we will need the means to defeat the enemy," Cleo stated as she tried to reason with him.

"Captain Joaquim and I plan to come out of our retirement. We will use the force again just like we did when we had just started together," Jimmy said as he walked down the stairs to join the conversation.

"Fredrick, you're also going to be a part of the mission," Joaquim told him.

Fredrick nodded.

"Do I have your support, Cleo? I can't go on this mission to save the Oba of Benoni without you. I need you by my side," Joaquim said.

"How can I let you go alone? You can barely figure out maps these days," Cleo stated sarcastically.

Joaquim smiled as he knew it was Cleo's way of caving in.

JOAQUIM STARTED TRAINING again. He believed he'd gotten rusty after retirement, which made him spend the following nights training while everyone else slept.

Cleo returned to planning a strategy for their mission. They relied on the old map of Benoni that Joaquim had drawn years ago with Lushinna's help.

Whenever Cleo went through the map, she sensed a strange familiarity with the land. It felt like she had an old connection with the place but couldn't figure it out.

The mercenaries left after Pedro's departure and were prepared for their new mission. Fredrick was satisfied with the progress of the crew. He was assigned to lead them to Benoni. He was excited because this was going to be his first mission.

A few hours before leaving for the mission, Joaquim looked for Jimmy to speak with him alone. He went to Jimmy's chamber to find him pacing up and down.

"You wanted to speak with me?" Jimmy asked.

"Yes. You will stay behind while we go ahead with the mission," Joaquim informed Jimmy, who was left stunned.

"How-"

"This matter concerns my family. The African Queen needs you in case something happens to us," Joaquim explained.

Jimmy was going to argue, but he saw the determined look on Joaquim's face.

"Aye, Captain..." Jimmy answered.

IT HAD BEEN TWO YEARS since the coup. Ookpala was still imprisoned, but his health had improved, and he managed to stay sane. Omo was the only person who visited him regularly and tried to keep him connected with the world outside prison.

Omo was known for his kind-hearted and merciful nature. He had a habit of helping people who needed assistance. He would often smuggle extra food from the palace's kitchen and give it to Oba Ookpala and the other prisoners.

Sometimes, Omo would get caught, but it was hard to stay angry at him since he had an air of childish cheerfulness. Omo could always see the light in the dark, which helped him hope for better days in Benoni.

"Do you remember the person who brought you to the palace?" Ookpala asked him one day.

"It was Chief Maina. I was about seven years old. I cannot remember the details. I just remember that before I came to the palace, I lived with my two brothers and my parents," Omo told him.

"If only we could get Maina to talk more about your past," Ookpala sighed.

"He guards the details with his life," Omo said as he tried to laugh.

"Ookpala wondered if Omo was the replaced son from Maina's household." He, however, chose to remain silent.

One day, Omo came running for Ookpala, who was sleeping at that time. It was early in the morning when Omo woke up Ookpala.

"Did Maina die?" Ookpala asked, rubbing his eyes.

"Even better," Omo said.

"What?"

"The African Queen has heard our plea. They will be arriving here to rescue you very soon," Omo told Ookpala.

"How will they fight an entire army of Benoni?" Ookpala wondered.

"Mishkia told me that they have taken on worse enemies," Omo said.

After a long time of suffering, Ookpala finally had hope. He longed for the day the African Queen would reach Benoni to rescue him. But he couldn't figure out why they were willing to risk themselves to rescue an imprisoned Oba.

Chapter 21: Homecoming

OOKPALA HEARD FOOTSTEPS approaching his cell. He was too tired to turn around and see who was coming. Ookpala had been held captive by Omonoma for a long time. He had gotten old and weak after his confinement.

"I hope you're enjoying your time down here," a familiar voice said.

Ookpala tilted his head to see who was speaking. It was Esoha. He had an evil smirk on his face. He would rarely visit Ookpala in the dungeon, but when he did, he made sure that he humiliated Ookpala.

"Would you like to join as well?" Ookpala asked coldly.

"I would never be in your place," Esoha said.

"You can never have my place, traitor," Ookpala shrugged.

"You could have simply declared Omonoma as your legitimate heir to the throne and saved yourself all this trouble," Esoha remarked.

"And you should have poisoned yourself before betraying Benoni," Ookpala stated as he raised his voice.

When Esoha began to leave, he was met by Omo, who stared at him sharply.

"Are you here to sing a lullaby to your old Oba? Esoha asked, grinning.

"I would sing one to you too if you like," Omo said dismissively.

Esoha rolled his eyes and walked away from the dungeon. Omo had brought food for Ookpala, which was concealed in a cloth bag that he carried with him everywhere.

"I brought the gravy you're so fond of," Omo said excitedly.

"I don't feel like having food," Ookpala stated, lying down on the ground.

"You have been eating less for a while. You can't allow yourself to get weak. We have a long battle ahead," Omo said.

"Do you think I should abdicate my right to the throne in favor of Omonoma?" Ookpala asked.

Omo stared at Ookpala, who looked like he was going to surrender. His eyes appeared tired, and his shoulders slumped. Omo could barely recognize the man that was once the Oba of Benoni.

"We must wait for the African Queen to arrive. People are going to rescue you, and you'll be the Oba again," Omo insisted.

"One day, I'll have to abdicate the throne," Ookpala said.

"Today is not that day," Omo stated firmly.

JOAQUIM STOOD AT THE deck of the boat carrying him and his crew. The crew was standing by, ready for him to give the cue to start marching toward the palace.

"Now," Joaquim said.

The crew descended from the boat, making their way through the thick bushes and toward the Red Palace. Cleo and the group had concealed their identities with masks. She marched along with Joaquim.

"There is the gate. We need to be vigilant," Cleo said.

The African Queen's crew had planned to climb the Red Palace's boundary walls as the guards stood there, protecting the gate of the Red Palace.

As the crew inched closer, Cleo stopped suddenly.

They could hear the guards speaking in the Benoni language.

"What happened?" Joaquim asked.

"I don't know why, but I can understand their language!" Cleo was perplexed.

Cleo looked around and stared at the place that appeared so familiar. She had started to get flashbacks once again. Everything looked so similar to what she saw in her nightmares.

It was the same place that Cleo had dreamed of for years. The bushes seemed as if she had been inside them. The Red Palace appeared as if she had lived there in her previous life.

"We need to keep moving, Cleo. This is not the time. I will explain everything later. "Joaquim realized that Cleo was regaining her memories. "I will confess to her as soon as I have restored her as Queen of Benoni." He vowed to himself.

Cleo couldn't understand what was happening either. She was supposed to keep moving, yet the palace's familiarity had started confusing her, and she was losing her pace.

"I do not understand what is happening to me. But I seem to remember this place. I do not know if it's from my dreams or old memories," Cleo said softly.

Suddenly, Cleo returned to reality. She looked at Joaquim, who was keenly reaching his hand out to her. The crew had started to climb the wall. Cleo also climbed the wall and they reached the inside of the Red Palace's outer courtyard. There was no one in sight which confused Joaquim.

"Where are the guards?" Joaquim wondered.

As soon as Joaquim spoke, a man grabbed him from behind and trapped him. When his crew started to run toward him to help him, an entire crowd emerged out of nowhere. The guards had masked their presence by painting their bodies with the red mud of the Red Palace.

"Leave him!" Cleo screamed.

One of the guards hit Cleo on her head with the butt of his whip, and she fell, hitting her head a second time on the wall as she collapsed to the ground, losing consciousness.

It was apparent that the Red Palace guards had been anticipating the attack and were waiting for Joaquim's crew to arrive. The old fox Esoha had been watching Omo's every move.

The rest of Joaquim's crew also jumped inside the Red Palace, and a huge fight broke out between the enemies.

Old Joaquim hadn't forgotten combat. He stabbed the man grabbing him with his dagger, and managed to break free of his grip. Joaquim ran toward Cleo, who was being held by two men. When he tried to stab them with his dagger, another man got hold of him and pushed him to the ground.

As Joaquim was about to get stabbed, Fredrick ran and got hold of the dagger in Joaquim's attacker's hand. Fredrick's hand was injured and he started bleeding as he tried to stop the attacker from stabbing Joaquim.

Fredrick was occupied with the man when another one marched toward him, holding a short and sharp spear in his hand. Joaquim spotted him aiming for Fredrick's head and got up back to his feet. As the man attempted to attack Fredrick, Joaquim pushed Fredrick out of the way, managing to get in the way, but he couldn't shield himself.

Joaquim fell to the ground with a loud thud. Fredrick turned around to find his grandfather bleeding profusely. The attacker had stabbed Joaquim in his chest with the spear, which was protruding from his chest. The short spear still remained stuck in his chest. He had taken the blade that was meant for Fredrick.

The Red Palace's guards overpowered the African Queen's crew. Fredrick, Cleo, and Joaquim were all captured by the guards. They were taken to the dungeons, where the prisoners were kept. The guards neglected to unmask the intruders as they were hurrying to drop them off in the dungeon and return to the fighting if any remained.

Ookpala was sleeping when he heard several steps rushing toward the dungeon, and he woke up immediately. The Red Palace guards were carrying several men and a woman. One of them was bleeding, and his blood stained the floor. They were ditched in the dungeon, and then the guards headed back to the battlefield.

"What happened to that man?" Ookpala asked the prisoners about Joaquim.

Fredrick was clinging to Joaquim, crying while keeping his hand on the wound, but the bleeding wouldn't stop. At about that same time, Cleo regained consciousness. As she did, more of her memories flooded in on her. She began to remember that Benoni was part of her history.

She looked around, and the pain of seeing her twin sons lying unnaturally on the ground pierced through her like it just happened a few hours ago.

She stared at Joaquim in shock. She realized that Joaquim was not her husband. She assessed the graveness of their situation. The familiarity of her environment and Joaquim's comment before the fighting that he would explain everything to her suddenly made sense. She made a split-moment decision.

Not giving further attention to her recovered memories, she leaned in and held Joaquim's head on her lap, unable to hold back her tears. It was clear that any attempt to remove the spear from Joaquim's chest would immediately cause him to bleed faster to his death.

"We need something to stop the bleeding immediately, or he will bleed to death," Ookpala told the prisoners.

Omo and Mishkia had reached the dungeon upon hearing the noise in the Red Palace. Mishkia saw the prisoners and knew they belonged to the African Queen but chose to keep quiet.

"Omo, bring something to stop the bleeding!" Ookpala screamed.

Omo ran back to get supplies while Mishkia remained in the dungeon. She was watching Joaquim bleeding, but she couldn't go inside as the dungeon was locked, for the guard with the keys was in the courtyard, defending the palace. All she could do was stand outside the cell and watch.

Omo returned from his corner with bandages and a couple of bottles of herbal medicine.

"Try to wrap this around the wound," Omo said as he gave Ookpala a piece of cloth dampened with an ointment.

Ookpala rushed to bandage Joaquim's wound. He tore Joaquim's shirt open and what he saw didn't look good. Joaquim had a deep wound, and blood kept oozing out from it. Ookpala knew that Joaquim was not going to survive.

"You're going to be fine," Ookpala lied as he tried to give Joaquim some hope.

"You think?" Joaquim retorted, and then he grinned with visible tears in his eyes.

When Ookpala finished dressing Joaquim's wound, he went back to his corner to let Joaquim spend his last moments with his companions.

Joaquim knew he was not going to see the light of day. There was no hope left for him, but he didn't want to leave the world before telling Cleo the truth about his past. He wanted to be fair, so he had to make a decision.

"I'm not going to live much longer, Cleo. There is something you need to know," Joaquim said.

"You'll have plenty of time to tell me whatever you want. Please don't lose hope, do not speak. Save your energy," Cleo pleaded.

"You were never raped. You're not Cleo," Joaquim finally confessed with tears rolling down his face.

"I know, I remember. I really would like you to tell me in your own words, when and why. However, this is not the time nor the place. Save your energy." Cleo had tears running down her face.

"I lied about your past when you woke up from the coma. You're not Cleo. You were not raped. You were brought to me so I could rescue you from a grave fate awaiting you. I love Pedro. He'll always be my son, but he is not the result of a rape." Joaquim told her.

Cleo was shattered. She couldn't believe what she was hearing and didn't want to believe it either. But her memories were returning and he was only confirming what she now remembered.

"My love, you're not in your senses. I don't want to hear what you're saying." Cleo said tearfully. "You are delirious. Please reserve your energy."

"He's telling you the truth," Mishkia interrupted, standing right outside the cell.

"What do you know about me? Shut up!" Cleo screamed!

"I'm the Palace Head Maid! I was the one who brought you to Joaquim," Mishkia told Cleo.

"What is happening? I don't understand..." Cleo stammered. She felt like she was starting to lose her mind. Some of her memories were intact, and some were fragmented.

"You are Queen Iredia of Benoni. This was your home before the council of the Red Palace came after you as a part of their conspiracy to kill you along with your twin sons. You were pregnant when you were attacked. Your son, Pedro is the rightful heir to the throne," Mishkia stated.

"My twin sons!" Cleo was shaking. Mishkia's account was rapidly filling in the gaps for her.

Images of two dead boys flashed in front of Cleo's eyes. She began thinking about the nightmares she had for decades where there were always two children, bushes, and a snake.

"You were married to Oba Ookpala and had identical twin boys with him, which was a bad omen for Benoni. The conspirators schemed to kill your children, and they ended up poisoning them with soup. You managed to escape with my help. You were on top of the tree outside in the bushes when a snake bit you. I sucked out the poison and gave you medicine to tackle the venom. I had suffered a similar snake bite weeks before your attack, and Dr. Anita of the African Queen had given me some medicine to combat snake venom. You would have been killed if you stayed in Benoni, so I took you to Captain Joaquim," Mishkia narrated the past of Cleo.

Cleo was left speechless as her memories bombarded her mind. She didn't know how to react or what to say. She had lived her life puzzled about the reoccurring nightmares of dead children, thinking that she had everything she had wished for, only to find out that Joaquim was a scumbag who had been lying to her all along.

She finally remembered everything after Mishkia's narrative and her regaining partial memories after being hit in the courtyard.

"I saw Joaquim break apart after Lushinna. I chose Joaquim to look after you because I knew he was never going to let anything bad happen to you. You were safe with him," Mishkia explained.

"I have always loved you, Cleo. You brought me back to life. It broke me to keep the truth from you, but I couldn't risk Pedro suffering the same fate as your twin sons. Also, I was selfish. I did not want you to leave me. Please forgive me for taking your identity," Joaquim sobbed as he began to cough up some blood.

Fredrick and Ookpala rushed over to Cleo. Ookpala started shaking as he heard Mishkia's revelations.

Cleo could remember everything that had occurred. For the first time in decades, the memories that had vanished were as clear as day in her mind.

Cleo knew that Joaquim was not going to make it. She felt betrayed after discovering the truth, but then she reminded herself of how Joaquim had taken care of her. Joaquim loved her selflessly, and she couldn't deny it.

She refused to let their last moments be tainted with anger and unforgiveness. She could not let this lover of so many years leave the world heartbroken. She chose to grant him her forgiveness.

"I forgive you," Cleo said with tears streaming down her face.

"You have given me the greatest joy in life. I wouldn't have lived this long if it weren't for you. I was so happy with you, which made me selfish. I didn't want to lose you, so I kept the truth from you. I did not know how to explain the fact that Pedro was a full-bloodied African, hence I lied that you were raped. You have every reason to despise me," Joaquim said, broken.

"I don't despise you. I have always loved you with all my heart. I forgive you." Cleo told Joaquim.

"Mishkia! You?" Ookpala seemed to be having trouble with his words.

"Your Oba Ookpala mourned you for years. He refused to name a successor for the throne since he didn't want to give anyone the right that belonged to your children," Mishkia looked at Oba Ookpala in shame. "He preferred death over naming an heir who was not right."

"Why didn't you tell us that earlier?" Cleo asked.

"I couldn't steal you from Joaquim after everything he had gone through, so I stayed quiet," Mishkia said, with her eyes pleading for understanding.

"But you could steal from me?" Ookpala finally found his voice.

Cleo started thinking about her nightmares. She had remembered her past life. She could finally see the faces of her dead twins. All the memories were coming back to her now, including the ones when she had told Ookpala that she was bearing his child right before her twins were murdered.

Cleo began to sob uncontrollably. Lifting both hands to her ears, she sobbed loudly. The sound of her crying reached Ookpala's ears. He heard her sobs deep in his soul. He felt like he was seeing it all from a far place, for he had gone into a daze. He was witnessing the whole situation unfold, astonished by the turn of events.

He looked up at Fredrick, who suddenly took off his mask.

Ookpala was surprised to find a young man who looked exactly like him but was almost white. Cleo also took off her mask, leaving Ookpala short for words.

Ookpala fell to his knees as he saw the face of his beloved Iredia!

This was the love of his life that he had finally buried a few years prior to his imprisonment. She had not changed a lot over the years; her eyes remained the same. It was her eyes that had attracted him to her at the beginning of their match.

"He's your Oba Ookpala," Mishkia told Cleo.

"Iredia? Am I dreaming?" Ookpala asked, touching her hands reverently.

Cleo lifted her hand and touched Ookpala's face, nodding her head as she tried to choke back her sobs unsuccessfully.

"It's me, My Prince. How long did your coronation last? How long have I been unconscious? Unaware of my life? Adrift without a thought for my husband or children? They killed Peter and Paul. Peter! Paul! Oh-Oh. O-k-p-a-l-a!" she broke down sobbing afresh.

Ookpala and Iredia hugged each other. Iredia realized the years she had lost could have been spent with her husband. They were both in their sixties. They had spent most of their lives apart.

She began to explain everything that had happened since the last time they saw each other.

"Our unborn son is now a man. His name is Pedro. Fredrick, here, is our grandson."

As she narrated her story to Oba Ookpala and an astonished Fredrick, Joaquim breathed his last, and both Iredia and Fredrick burst out into fresh bouts of tears for the deceased Captain who had given them his heart.

Chapter 22: Blood Line

MAINA HAD A GRAY BEARD that reached his chest. His hands had started shaking with age, yet he remained firmly seated in the council. He had managed to groom Omonoma over the years, twisting the youth into despising his father, Oba Ookpala.

It was during the early hours of the morning when the doors of Omonoma's chamber were pushed open by Maina. Omonoma was studying scripts, seated comfortably in his chair, when he heard Maina coming in.

"We need to sort the matter," Maina said.

"I told you I didn't want to discuss the matter until tomorrow," Omonoma retorted, frustrated.

"It's already tomorrow and you need to realize the urgency of it," Maina argued. Old Maina's influence over Omonoma was undeniable, and he never refused him.

"You want me to reach a decision to execute my father to ensure the legitimacy of my throne. I'm aware," Omonoma stated, exhausted.

"It's not what I want. It's what needs to be done. You cannot be a legitimate Oba as long as Ookpala is alive. Benoni has always functioned this way. A son only ascends to the throne when the father is deceased. In your case, the rightful owner of the throne is still alive and rotting in a dungeon," Maina explained. He went on as he sat on Omonoma's bed, where he rarely slept.

"How does it affect me if he's in the dungeon? He can't challenge my authority as long as he's there. He's a prisoner of the Obadom. He has no grounds to pose a threat to my throne," Omonoma said as he stood up.

"The Red Palace has already been attacked, and it's only a matter of time until Ookpala manages to break free with the aid of our enemies. You are forgetting the rebels are roaming the streets of Benoni, and they're prepared to wage war against your throne once Ookpala gets out," Maina pointed out.

"Is there anything else that can be done besides execution?" Omonoma asked.

"Why? Are you afraid to sentence him to death? The same man who never accepted your legitimacy or looked after you?" Maina questioned harshly as he stood up.

"I simply want to know if we have any other choices. I don't want to risk aggravating the people of Benoni," Omonoma expressed his concern and looked the other way.

"Of course, you're concerned about the people of Benoni," Maina said sarcastically. "There is something that can be done."

"Now will be a great time to tell me about it," Omonoma stated. He sounded frustrated by Maina's antics.

"Ookpala can cede the throne. This will give you rightful legitimacy for the throne." Maina told Omonoma.

"We have been working on that for two years," Omonoma said, sounding hopeless.

"Try it again! I'll leave that task to you. I wish you the best of luck with your quest."

Maina smirked as he walked out of Omonoma's chambers. Omonoma couldn't go back to sleep after Maina left. He kept pacing his chamber and thinking about how he could persuade Ookpala to cede the throne.

IN THE AFTERNOON, OMONOMA decided to visit Ookpala in his dungeon. He wore his father's silk robe and headed there. When he reached the gate, he demanded Ookpala be brought to him as he didn't want to go inside his cell.

Ookpala was brought before Omonoma, tied in chains. Ookpala refused to look Omonoma in the eye as he stood in front of him.

"I have come here with a proposal for you. It can serve you well if you agree," Omonoma said.

Ookpala said nothing, remaining indifferent to Omonoma's words.

"I don't want you to remain imprisoned in the dungeon. I have the authority to grant you freedom, and I want to do that regardless of how you have treated me my entire life. All you have to do is cede the throne, and I'll set you free," Omonoma stated.

"Why? Because you don't have the courage to kill me?" Ookpala asked snidely.

"I don't wish to kill you. You're my father," Omonoma said as his hands shook.

"You're no son of mine. I thought you were god Otun's son from the abominable coronation. However, I now know that you are not even god Otun's son. You are a nameless bastard.

"I would suggest you kill me because I'm not going to give up the throne to you !" Ookpala yelled.

Feeling crushed, Omonoma refrained from saying anything and gestured for the guards to escort Ookpala back to the dungeon. As Omonoma turned to leave the dungeon, he spotted a young interracial man kept in the cell who looked incredibly similar to Ookpala. Omonoma was unaware of his identity, but he was taken aback by the striking resemblance to his Oba Ookpala.

"Should we leave?" a guard asked as he interrupted Omonoma, who kept staring at the man.

Omonoma nodded, and wordlessly, he left for the Red Palace with bowed shoulders.

Chapter 23: A White Oba

AS SOON AS HE RETURNED to his chamber, Omonoma asked for Esoha to be summoned.

"You asked for me, my Oba?" Esoha said as he entered the chamber.

"That white man in the dungeon... Esoha, he resembles my father so much. Who is he?" Omonoma asked.

"Which man? Are you talking about the ones who attacked the Red Palace?" Esoha inquired.

"Yes. Didn't you see that man's face?"

"They had their masks on when we brought them to the dungeon," Esoha explained.

"I want you to find out about those invaders. Who are they, and why did they attack the Red Palace? I don't think it's as simple as it looks," Omonoma ordered.

Esoha nodded and left the chamber.

MISHKIA WAS STANDING at the gate of the Old Palace when she saw Omo. He was carrying food for Ookpala like he usually did around that time.

"Omo, come with me," Mishkia whispered.

Omo followed Mishkia to the courtyard of the Old Palace. She found a corner that wasn't easily visible to everyone else and gestured for Omo to stand beside her.

"Keep an eye out for anyone who roams here. We need to be careful. Omonoma can't find the truth about Queen Iredia and her grandson. He will slaughter them the minute he finds out about their identity. You're aware that he's thirsty for power and will go to any extent to achieve what he desires," Mishkia explained to Omo.

"How long can we keep it down? I fear that sooner or later, they're going to discover the truth," Omo stated while looking out for intruders around him and Mishkia.

Mishkia heard a thud and turned around to see if anyone else was also present there. She couldn't see anyone there and took it for slight confusion. After Mishkia and Omo left, a man emerged from the shadows and went in the direction of the Red Palace.

IT WAS DURING THE WEE hours of the morning when a boat stopped at the shore of Benoni. A man draped in cloth all over his body stepped down from the boat.

"You are finally here in Benoni," another man said. He was waiting for him as he extended his arms in an embrace.

"Yes, Shomar, and I am here on urgent matters," the draped man said. He removed the drape covering his face to reveal his identity. It was Jimmy. He embraced Shomar and patted his shoulders.

"How can I be of service to you?" Shomar asked.

"I need someone who can get me to the Red Palace," Jimmy explained as they walked toward a brick house.

"I know someone who can help you, but what business do you have in the Red Palace?" Shomar asked, concerned.

"My captain, Captain Joaquim, and his wife arrived here recently, but they haven't returned yet. I need to know what happened to them."

"I will bring the person who can help you in the morning. But first, you need to rest," Shomar said.

Shomar led Jimmy into his house. He gave him a bowl of warm soup and showed him the place where he was supposed to sleep. The next morning, Jimmy was awoken by Shomar. He realized that he wasn't alone. There was someone else accompanying him.

"Omo, this is my old and dear friend, Jimmy. I owe everything to him. He helped me when everyone else left me. I want you to help him," Shomar told Omo.

"Shomar tells me that you need to get inside the Red Palace," Omo stated as he extended his hand, and Jimmy shook it.

"Yes. Do you think you can sneak me inside?" Jimmy asked.

"It's risky since it has recently come under attack, so the guards are very careful right now," Omo explained.

"An attack?" Jimmy asked.

"Yes. The palace was attacked, and the ones who instigated it were captured."

"Captured?" Jimmy said with foreboding.

"Yes. Do you know about Captain Joaquim and his wife? The couple from the African Queen?" Omo asked.

"I have heard of the African Queen," Jimmy edged carefully.

As Omo explained to Jimmy what had happened on the ill-fated night when the crew of the African Queen attacked the Red Palace, Jimmy revealed he was a sailor of the African Queen.

Omo told him about how the prisoners were captured and where they were taken. Omo didn't have the courage to tell Jimmy about Joaquim's death, so he left out that part.

Together, Omo and Jimmy planned how they were going to help the prisoners escape the dungeon. Omo explained to him where the guards were stationed and the best way to get through them.

"We must hurry because the guards are going to get changed soon, and we have to make it just in time to get the prisoners out," Omo told Jimmy.

Omo helped Jimmy sneak into the Red Palace. Although they entered the place in broad daylight, no one spotted them as they had disguised themselves as the guards.

Jimmy followed Omo through a hidden corridor that apparently only a few people in the palace knew about. The corridor took them straight to the dungeon where the guards were stationed.

"What do we do now?" Jimmy asked in a whisper.

"We wait for them to move," Omo said.

"Or we can slice their throats," Jimmy suggested.

"We can't-"

Before Omo could stop Jimmy, he had already started running to where the guards were standing. There were only two on duty, and Jimmy managed to grab one from behind and stabbed him in the skull.

When the other guard saw Jimmy, he took out his machete and ran to strike him but Omo was able to get a hold of him, grabbing both of his hands as Jimmy slit the guard's throat.

"Inside," Jimmy gestured to Omo.

The pair stopped when they heard the rustling sound of footsteps running toward them. Apparently, Jimmy hadn't been as subtle as he'd hoped with his tricks to sneak in.

"Jimmy, you need to escape, or they will slaughter you," Omo told him as they made their way back to the corridor.

"I can't run away. I need to see Captain Joaquim. How can I leave when he is imprisoned in Benoni's dungeon?"

"He's free," Omo said.

"What do you mean?" Jimmy asked, perplexed.

"Joaquim didn't make it. He did not survive the attack."

Jimmy's world changed in a matter of seconds. The man he had come to rescue was no longer alive, and the guards were chasing him.

"What about Cleopatra and Fredrick?" He held back his tears as Omo helped him sneak out of the palace.

"They are alive. Omo assured him."

QUEEN IREDIA WAS LYING in a corner of the dungeon. The guards had carried out Joaquim's body after they found out that he had died. She couldn't stop thinking about what they must have done to the body. She wanted to give him a proper burial, but instead, she was stuck in a dungeon.

During the last two days, Iredia found out that the man she had loved all her life wasn't her husband yet stayed by her side faithfully, and the one who was her husband had been unfaithful to her. While their sons were being slaughtered, he'd been busy bedding four women, even siring a son with one of them.

She'd found out about Omonoma and how Ookpala had bedded the virgin priestesses while she was carrying his child, Pedro. She felt betrayed by Ookpala's infidelity. While she'd been running for her life and had lost the twins, Ookpala had been bedding four priestesses! She couldn't let go of his lack of virtue during these testing times.

After all, it was Ookpala's infidelity that had become the reason for his imprisonment. If he had listened to her when she did not want to leave Yola and had refused to be involved in the heinous customs, Omonoma would have never been born and seized Ookpala's throne.

Chapter 24: The Lost Queen of Benoni

SOMEONE KNOCKED ON the doors of Esoha's chambers. Esoha asked them to come inside. It was the same man who had been hiding in the shadows beside Mishkia and Omo.

"Did you find anything?" Esoha asked.

"Queen Iredia has returned," he said.

Esoha's eyes widened in surprise. He couldn't believe what he was hearing.

"What are you talking about, Ankeel?" Esoha asked. I saw her corpse! She could not have survived her fall from the tree.

"She is one of the prisoners who attacked the Red Palace. She has been alive all along, and she hasn't returned alone. She came back with her grandson, who is apparently a legitimate heir to the throne," Ankeel told Esoha.

Esoha's eyes bulged from his sockets.

"There is more. The heir to the throne is "oyinbo.""

What? Esoha grabbed a vase and threw it against the wall.

"He is white, more specifically, he is half-caste" Ankeel grinned.

He ran straight to Omonoma, who was occupied with his plants in the gardens of Red Palace. Omonoma seemed to be in a cheerful mood but Esoha had to break the news to him.

"My Oba, I come as the bearer of bad news," Esoha said, bowing his head down.

"Say it," Omonoma commanded without turning around.

"Oba Ookpala's wife, Queen Iredia, is alive and here."

Omonoma dropped the flower he was holding in his hands. He turned around. His eyes were red and his fists clenched.

"You're certain?" Omonoma asked.

"The prisoners in the dungeon are none other than Queen Iredia and Ookpala's grandson, Fredrick. He is apparently an heir to the throne. He is

Ookpala's grandson from the third son who was birthed by his Queen while she was lost."

Esoha shivered as he told Omonoma.

"Follow me to the dungeon right now," Omonoma ordered.

Omonoma, accompanied by Esoha and four guards, headed to the dungeon and marched up to the cell.

"Are you Iredia?" Omonoma asked her.

She was the only woman in the dungeon. Iredia didn't answer him. She knew who he was. She could see it in his eyes which were filled with rage.

"I have heard a strange rumor, and I hope it's not true. Some people say that you're the lost Queen of Benoni. They also say that you have returned with a rightful heir to the throne," Omonoma laughed.

Iredia chose to remain silent.

"Separate these scum of the earth from my dear father," Omonoma ordered the guards.

Iredia was dragged by the guards to a different cell, and Fredrick was dragged to another. The cells were far apart, so they couldn't find a way to talk.

The council meeting was called during the night. It was presided by Omonoma, who was accompanied by Maina and Esoha. All the heads of the different tribes of Benoni were present. They were clueless about what had transpired in the last two days.

"I apologize for disturbing your supper tonight, but we have an important issue at hand. I have found out that some of you have opinions about the legitimacy of my claim to the throne. I'm not here to punish you. I simply want to learn your doubts," Omonoma said.

They stayed silent, feeling nervous to voice what was on their mind.

"Odunsi," Omonoma called out to one of the chiefs in the council. "Why don't you share your thoughts with us?"

"We have learned about the arrival of Oba Ookpala's grandson in Benoni. We believe that he should be the rightful Oba as he is the legitimate heir to the throne," Odunsi told Omonoma.

"Is there any evidence that he is the rightful heir to the throne? How do we know that he's Oba Ookpala's heir other than taking their word for it?" Omonoma argued.

"Well, there is no doubt to the legitimacy. I have seen him, and he is the spitting image of Oba Ookpala," Odunsi expressed.

"Except that he is white. Benoni cannot have a white Oba. The tradition of this land doesn't allow for a white Oba to ascend the throne," Omonoma laughed.

"He is the blood of Oba Ookpala," Odunsi stated, feeling conflicted by Omonoma's words.

Suddenly, Omonoma stood up aggressively, which prompted Odunsi to return to his seat.

"I can see where your loyalty lies, Chief Odunsi. Whoever this person and his mother are, they will serve the consequences of the chaos they have caused in Benoni. You cannot just show up in Benoni and claim to be the heir to the throne," Omonoma told everyone.

The council thought it better to stay silent than argue with Omonoma, who seemed to have visibly lost his senses. The vein in his neck was throbbing and he was thumping his fists on the table.

"Queen Iredia and her white grandson will be executed in the town square as soon as possible. I want all of Benoni to witness what happens to those who challenge their Oba," Omonoma declared.

"It will only be suitable to execute them after the New Yam Festival, which will take seven days to finish. We aren't supposed to spill blood during the festival," Maina intervened.

"Very well. They will be executed right after the festival ends. Anyone who resists the sentencing and tries to challenge it will be executed as well," Omonoma said before leaving the council meeting.

IT WAS PAST MIDNIGHT when four men entered the cell where Fredrick was kept. They covered Fredrick's head with a sack and bound his hands with a rope. Then he was taken out of the palace.

Fredrick couldn't see what was happening, but he could hear the noise in his surroundings. The men were negotiating with someone. After they were done talking, Fredrick was taken into a building and locked in a room.

The men returned to Maina's chamber, who was still awake and sitting on his bed.

"What did you get in return?" Maina asked.

"Cowries and decoratives," a man answered.

"Well, not a bad price for that useless boy," Maina said.

Maina had been leading a group of slave traders who operated in Benoni. He had been the leader of the slave traders for about four decades, yet no one from the Red Palace had ever discovered his activities. Fredrick was just one of many prisoners from the dungeon who had been sold that night.

IT WAS EARLY IN THE morning when Omo was walking past Omonoma's chamber, and he spotted Maina walking about. He was surprised because Maina usually spent the early morning in his chamber. It was an unusual hour for the visit.

Right before Omo was about to exit the hallway, he saw Omonoma emerging from his chamber. He was dressed in a gray silk robe and appeared rather content with himself.

Omonoma arrived in the Great Hall unaccompanied. He looked around and saw many faces that had undermined his authority the last time he addressed the council.

"Why does he look so pleased? Something is wrong?" Chief Odunsi said to the chief sitting next to him.

"I'm delighted to be here and see all the friendly faces who supported me faithfully the last time we were here," Omonoma said to the council.

"I have some sad news for those who were rooting for the coronation of the lost imposter queen's alleged grandson. Last night, the beloved imposter queen tried to escape the dungeons after stealing valuables from the Red Palace. She wasn't alone in her heist. Her grandson was participating as well," Omonoma said with composure.

The council was taken aback by the sudden turn of events. People in the council started whispering to each other, causing unrest in the Great Hall.

"Hold your precious tongue or I will chop it like I'm going to do with your dear lost queen!" Omonoma yelled.

A deadly silence took over the council, and no one dared to speak.

"The imposter queen was caught last night during her escape, but Fredrick managed to flee. We can no longer wait for the execution. She has tried to escape before, and she will try again. Her execution will take place the very next morning after the Yam Festival ends," Omonoma announced before leaving the Great Hall.

Omo was lurking in a corner, listening to the entire address. He slid into the shadows when Omonoma left the Great Hall.

Chapter 25: Rescued

"OMO WISHES TO SEE YOU," a chamber maid informed Esoha.

"Let him in," Esoha said.

"To what do I owe the honor of your appearance?" Esoha said mockingly as soon as Omo entered the chamber.

"I bring a message from Oba Ookpala," Omo said.

"I'm all ears," Esoha invited him, sitting in a chair.

"Ookpala wants to have supper with both Omonoma and his wife, Queen Iredia, at his side," Omo informed Esoha.

"Very well. I will see what can be done," Esoha told Omo.

BEFORE OMONOMA COULD head back to his chamber, Esoha came running after him and stopped him midway.

"Oba!" Esoha called out.

"Who set you lose?" Omonoma asked.

"We need to speak," Esoha said, panting.

"Say it already," Omonoma ordered. He didn't like waiting.

"He's ready to cede his throne," Esoha said.

"I want Maina," Omonoma commanded.

Not long after, Maina was summoned to the balcony of Omonoma's chamber, where Esoha was present as well.

"What's happening?" Maina asked as soon as he saw Omonoma speaking to Esoha.

"Ookpala is ready to cede the throne," Omonoma informed Maina.

"In exchange for?"

"He wants Iredia to be spared," Esoha told Maina.

"Of course, he wants his dear wife to be spared," Maina scoffed.

"This is what we wanted," Omonoma said, appearing content.

"You shouldn't trust him too easily. I have spent a great deal of time with him and I know he's capable of changing his colors," Maina warned Omonoma.

"It's the succession I care about, not him," Omonoma explained.

"As long as that woman is alive, the Red Palace is at risk of rebellion. You need to make a calculated play." Maina said.

"What should be our strategy?" Omonoma asked.

"We spare Iredia for the show. Once Ookpala cedes his throne, she will be finished," Maina told Omonoma.

"That can cause a rebellion," Esoha expressed his concern.

"Not if no one finds out about what happened," Maina said.

AFTER A MISERABLE TIME in the dungeon, Ookpala was dressed in the old robes he wore when he was the Oba of Benoni. He walked to the supper accompanied by Omo and under the watchful eyes of Esoha.

Omonoma arrived shortly after Ookpala and sat at the head of the table. It was the first time he was going to have supper with his father, something he had never done before. Omonoma was followed by Iredia, who wore a purple gown. Ookpala looked at his wife, who was wearing the same color as the first time he saw her.

When everyone was seated in the chairs, Omonoma reached for his calabash of palm wine and raised it in the air.

"To my father and his queen," Omonoma said, looking directly into Ookpala's eyes.

As soon as Ookpala raised the toast, Omonoma's guards intruded on the supper and seized him.

"What are you doing?" Omonoma screamed at the men.

Omonoma was restrained by two men, and one of them held a dagger to his throat, not allowing him to move.

Iredia watched the entire situation unfold in astonishment. The guards then moved aside to make space for a man entering the dining hall. The man walked in slowly, striding in with his walking cane, which was obviously not a walking aid but a weapon in disguise. The head of the cane was a beautiful piece of art.

The man was Pedro!

Omonoma watched Pedro stand in front of him in horror. He couldn't believe what was happening to him. He had been betrayed by his own people.

"Who are you?"

"Take him," Captain Pedro commanded. Omonoma was dragged out of the dining hall without an explanation.

"Pedro," Iredia stated gladly as she hugged him. "What just happened?"

"Benoni owed us. The African Queen has helped rescue many of those who were the followers of Omonoma. We have rescued the families of his followers as well. It was time for them to return the favor," Pedro began explaining. "We hatched a strategy with Omonoma's followers. They transferred their loyalties to us. I reached here last night; we disarmed the guards and I had a meeting with Oba Ookpala."

"He is your biological father," Iredia corrected him.

"I'm proud of you, my son," Ookpala told Pedro.

"You were aware?" Iredia asked.

"Yes. I found out about father and Oba Ookpala before I made it to the dungeon from Uncle Jimmy," Pedro explained.

AS SOON AS OMONOMA was seized and thrown into the dungeon, the people of Benoni rejoiced as they found that their Oba had returned to the throne. This time, Benoni finally had its queen back. Iredia was declared the queen of Benoni, and order was restored at last.

Ookpala commanded the council meeting to be held as he wanted to address them. He ordered Esoha's and Maina's people to also join them.

"I want to know what happened to Efe. He has been kept away from me for a long time, and I wish to know where he is now," Ookpala announced.

One of Esoha's men stepped forward with his head bowed down.

"Efe was imprisoned in the dungeon as well but at a different location. After a few months of his imprisonment, Efe became ill, and his health declined. The healers couldn't save him. He passed away a few months ago," he said.

Ookpala felt shattered as he found out that his loyal man was no more. He tried to hold back his emotions since he had other matters to address.

"I believe the council was told that Fredrick escaped, but if he had done that, why hasn't he returned after finding out that I have taken back the throne?" Ookpala asked.

"May I?" Omo asked.

"Yes," Ookpala said.

"I have found out that Fredrick in fact never escaped. He was taken from the dungeon and sold into slavery," Omo revealed.

"What? Who was behind it?" Ookpala asked.

"Maina and his people," Omo answered.

"How does he have connections with slave traders?" Ookpala asked.

Omo gestured at Mishkia, standing beside him, to come forward.

"You have something to tell me?" Ookpala asked.

"Maina is not only my husband, but also the leader of a group of slave traders. People from the Red Palace also worked for him and I'm one of them. We followed his orders. He traded slaves, focusing on buying and selling them. He has been doing so for decades now," Mishkia revealed.

"Then..." Ookpala started to say.

"No. I was not involved in Fredrick's disappearance. He was already sold before I was notified of it. Had I known, I would have done my best to prevent it," Mishkia said.

"This is horrible!" Ookpala could not stay still. He grabbed a pitcher and smashed it against the wall. "But we will get to the bottom of this matter in no time!"

Chapter 26: The Sons of the Oba

"ENOUGH!" MAINA SCREAMED as he was whipped with a lash for the twentieth time.

Maina was thrown into the dungeon after Omonoma was seized. Ookpala was furious at Maina and wanted him to suffer for the murder of his twins. He was constantly receiving torture from his captors, never getting a minute of respite.

Finally, he gave in.

"They're alive!" Maina managed to say as he screamed with pain.

"Who is alive?" the guard asked, dropping his hand that held the lash.

"Peter and Paul, Ookpala's twins. They were never killed," Maina said, sobbing with relief that the lashing had stopped, at least momentarily.

Ookpala was informed about the development. He left for the dungeons immediately to speak to Maina. When he arrived, he found a bloody Maina leaning against the wall of the dungeon.

"Tell him what you told us," the guard ordered.

"Your sons are alive," Maina said weakly as soon as he saw Ookpala entering the dungeon.

"You ordered for my children to be poisoned," Ookpala said.

"They were only drugged so they would remain unconscious while they were sold," Maina confessed.

"My children... sold as slaves! Who did you sell them to?" Ookpala asked furiously.

"They were sold to a slave trader on a plantation. I used to know about the whereabouts of Manasee-"

"Manasee?"

"Peter. His name was changed to Manasee just before he was sold. As for Paul, the trail went cold a few years ago and they stopped informing me," Maina said.

"Who else have you sold?" Ookpala questioned.

"Everyone you sentenced to death for any reason who was kept unsupervised in the dungeon. Random unsuspecting people who were in their farms alone at night. People without close family members. People with outstanding conflicts with members of my group. You see, it doesn't benefit anyone when someone dies. There are better ways to use human lives. Death is not profitable, Benoni was bloody, and lots of people were being killed," Maina explained.

"Where are they? Tell me now, you swine! Where are my twin boys?" Ookpala roared.

"You can't kill me now, can you? I'm not that easy. I can get them back for you, but you will have to spare me and Omonoma for that," Maina smirked with his bloodied mouth.

"You have nothing to gain from Omonoma anymore. Why are you so infatuated with him?" Ookpala asked cunningly as he remembered Ebere's confession to him while he was imprisoned.

He wanted Maina to confirm that so-called confession from Ebere, Mishkia's executed son.

"You're so naive for an Oba. Omonoma is my blood! Can't you see that?" Maina declared, and he started laughing like a maniac when he looked at the expression on Ookpala's face.

Ookpala stepped back, nodding his head.

"Your blood? Ebere was right. Explain yourself. Who is my so-called son, then? Where is god Otun's son?" Ookpala asked.

"What is the point? You will reject him anyway. He is god Otun's son, right?" Maina mocked him. "He's the one who feeds you and sings lullabies for you at night."

"Omo?"

"Yes, Omo. He was the one who was born by the priestess you bedded. She died during childbirth, and my wife had to be his wet nurse since she was already nursing Omonoma," Maina revealed.

"What have you done, Maina?" Ookpala asked.

"Exactly what you have done. I was looking out for my family. I would have sold Omo as well, but for his connection to god Otun. I did not want to invoke the wrath of god Otun. But, if you want to find out about the whereabouts of your children, you have to agree to my terms," Maina demanded.

"What are your terms?" Ookpala asked.

"Banishment instead of execution. You spare Omonoma and me. You can execute Mishkia, that betrayer of a wife, and I will lead you to your children," Maina stated as he tried to bargain.

Ookpala left the dungeon and headed toward the Old Palace. He marched to the palace with quick steps and his fists clenched.

"Ask Mishkia to see me," Ookpala commanded a maid.

When Mishkia arrived, she saw Ookpala furiously pacing around the hallway.

"My Oba, how can I be of service?"

"Why did you hide the truth from me?" Ookpala asked.

"What truth?" Mishkia replied.

"Omonoma is your son, not mine," Ookpala said.

Mishkia fell to her knees instantly as she struggled to look Ookpala in the eye.

"I couldn't refuse Maina. He doesn't allow resistance. I gave birth to Ebere as a teenager. Maina was unaware that he was my son when Omonoma sentenced him to death," Mishkia revealed.

"You and Maina have ruined Omonoma and Omo's childhood. You fed them lies!" Ookpala screamed.

"I just had a stillbirth when Maina brought Omo to me to be his wet nurse after his mother died during childbirth. Later, Maina and I adopted Omonoma as our child," Mishkia confessed through her tears. "Then, Maina had the idea to swap the babies. He wanted to have more power over the throne. Omo's full name is Omonoba. He is the son of the dead priestess. Omonoma was a baby that we found by the stream. We do not know his heritage. Whatever Maina did was a part of his strategy to usurp the throne one day."

"Maina deserves to be executed, but he's bargaining for his life with the information about my children," Ookpala sputtered.

Mishkia wasn't allowed to leave until a decision was reached about her fate. Ookpala was furious. He had trusted Mishkia with his life, only to discover that she had kept this terrible truth hidden.

"Maina didn't just commit treason, but he stole my life from me! I have been fed lies so others could achieve their purposes. My son has been kept away from me. How does one expect me to grant Maina banishment instead of a death sentence? In all of these confusions, how do I even begin to decipher the truth from the lies?" Ookpala asked, his voice trembling as he addressed her.

"I don't expect you to forgive us. We attempted treason and conspired to rob you of everything that belonged to you," Mishkia said. "But I beg you, have mercy."

"You might as well know then that the punishment for treason is death!" Ookpala yelled. He didn't appear to be receptive to Mishkia's situation, whose pleas for leniency were beginning to irritate him.

Ookpala stood up and left the chamber in the Old Palace. His guardsmen were awaiting him outside the gates of the palace. Ookpala abruptly stopped and turned to one of his guards.

"Arrest her. She is a traitor," Ookpala ordered the guard.

The guardsmen marched inside the Old Palace and grabbed Mishkia by her arms. Over the years, Mishkia had grown old and was unable to resist the arrest. She was aware of the consequences of the plot that she had made with Maina.

"Go ahead," Mishkia said to the guard, who hesitated to tie chains around her hands. "I am an accomplice in all this."

"I'm certain you will be released soon," the guard whispered in Mishkia's ear.

"I'm not certain about that," Mishkia said as she was arrested, accepting her fate and the punishment that came with it.

Chapter 27: The Royal Slave

IT WAS WAY PAST MIDNIGHT and everyone in the Red Palace was asleep. Ookpala cautiously left his chamber, wrapped in a gray shawl that was supposed to be worn by the servants of the palace. He ensured that Iredia was sleeping when he left his chamber since he didn't want her to discover what he was about to do.

Ookpala reached the dungeon cell where Maina was imprisoned. He had discussed his plan with the dungeon guards and they handed him the key to the cell.

"What brings you here, my Oba? Perhaps, you have reconsidered my terms?" Maina grinned viciously as he saw Ookpala approaching him.

Ookpala was beyond furious when he saw that smile. He was fuming with rage and marched straight toward Maina, who was clueless about Ookpala's motives.

"Wait-"

Before Maina could contemplate what was about to take place, Ookpala clenched his fist and punched Maina in the eye and he fell to the floor. Maina tried to get up, but Ookpala tightened his hands around his throat, trying to choke him.

"Please-," Maina begged.

Ookpala choked him with all his strength and Maina started to lose his breath. He coughed as Ookpala's grip tightened.

"Leave him," a voice ordered.

Ookpala let go of Maina. He was astounded when he found Iredia there, trying to force him to release his grip on Maina.

"He doesn't deserve to die in front of Benoni! He deserves to be killed right here, in the dungeon where he kept me for years!" Ookpala yelled.

"He is the last hope to finding our children. If he dies, we will never find out what happened to them," Iredia reasoned as she tried to persuade Ookpala, who was refusing to let go of Maina.

Finally, Ookpala loosened his grip around Maina's throat and shoved him away. Maina leaned against the wall behind him, gasping and coughing and trying to catch his breath.

Both Ookpala and Iredia left the dungeon. Ookpala was not happy about Iredia making him release Maina but he knew that she was trying to talk sense to him.

"He is a clever man. He knows he's playing with fire but won't give up hoping to escape the death sentence. You know better than anyone that he won't open his mouth until he's given some sort of assurance about his life," Iredia explained to Ookpala.

"So he gets to live after trying to kill you, my children, and keeping my son's identity from me?" Ookpala questioned as he stared at Iredia.

"We will see what we'll need to do once he leads us to our children. Until then, we have to arrange a royal pardon for him and exile him instead of giving him the death sentence," Iredia emphasized.

Ookpala stared in the distance as he tried to suppress his emotions. It was evident that he didn't want to lose hope of finding his children. After what seemed like an age, he forced himself to nod in agreement with Iredia's plan.

IT HAD BEEN SEVERAL days since Omonoma was imprisoned along with Maina and Mishkia. He had overheard the heated exchange between Ookpala and Maina, leading to him discovering his identity.

He had been quiet ever since, as he had nothing to say to Maina. His real father had kept his identity from him in his quest to control who would get to sit on the throne; he'd held back the truth, stopping him from embracing his identity.

One day, while the prisoners were temporarily out for air, Maina approached Omonoma after days of silence. He sat next to him and looked him in the eye.

"You would have done the same for your children," Maina told Omonoma, even though he'd said nothing.

"I don't know if I will let my children stray away from me to achieve my selfish motives," Omonoma responded. "I would not let them call another man their father."

"I wanted you to rule Benoni and you did. I'm proud of you, my son," Maina said, uttering the words that Omonoma had longed to hear all his life. "I have always made sure that I was around you. I raised you, taught you, and trained you for your future. You simply didn't know I was your father, but I always fulfilled my responsibility to you. I could not acknowledge that you were my biological child. Even Mishkia was not aware you were mine. But I gave you my all."

Omonoma nodded. He had always wondered what made Maina look out for him with such devotion. He never made him feel that he was missing his father.

"She's not going to forgive me, is she?" Omonoma asked after a while.

"For what?"

"Ebere," Omonoma said.

"No, she will not, nor will I forgive her for keeping the truth from me," Maina responded.

Omonoma was shattered that he had unknowingly killed his mother's son, Ebere. He'd sought her forgiveness for his decisions, but Mishkia refused to listen to him.

He thought to himself, "How well-suited Mishkia and Maina were to each other. Both keeping their biological children a secret from each other."

Mishkia had distanced herself from both Omonoma and Maina. She was disgusted by their conspiracies. She felt like Maina had been making a fool out of her in front of everyone. She was a grieving and angry mother. She didn't wish to be associated with either of them.

Mishkia was asleep in the open yard when she felt someone jerking her arm. She opened her eyes to find Maina holding her by her arm, preventing her from running away. He sat next to her, his eyes filled with rage.

"Wake up!" Maina whispered viciously.

"What is it?" Mishkia asked as she sat up on the floor.

"You have been trying to escape me, but not anymore. I have the right to know the truth. Why didn't you tell me the truth about Ebere's identity? When I married you, I was told that Ebere was Lushinna's son, your nephew and you had decided to look after him when she passed. Why couldn't you tell me he was your son?" Maina asked as he jerked Mishkia by her shoulders.

"God knows what you would have done to Ebere if you knew he was my blood but not yours! I did my best to protect him, and I don't owe you any justifications," Mishkia retorted as she tried to free herself from Maina's grip.

"You turned on me for Ookpala!" Maina spat.

"What about Omonoma and how you kept his identity from him? Was that fair?" Mishkia asked.

"I can do whatever I want with my blood!" Maina hissed at her.

"But-"

Mishkia stopped mid-sentence as she realized what Maina had just revealed. He'd told her that he was an orphaned, abandoned child they'd found. He'd been lying to her too!

"Who is the mother?" Mishkia asked, furious.

"That has nothing to do with you! All you should know is that she is a better woman than you," Maina responded.

"You take me for a fool which I'm not! It's written all over his face. Omonoma can't be anyone's son but yours. Wow! You made me believe he was picked up after being abandoned by the stream! He has inherited your cunningness. I have always known the truth. Your son killed mine! He stole my angel from me. I will never forgive him!" Mishkia declared as Maina began to walk away from the grieving mother.

"You should be afraid of your fate. Go to your idols and beg them to spare you. You won't be forgiven, Maina. Your son will suffer the same fate as mine did!" Mishkia screamed.

Maina stopped walking abruptly and turned back to Mishkia, who was screaming at him. His pursed lips formed a familiar vicious grin.

"Nothing can happen to me or my son. Ookpala is ready to negotiate the terms of my reprimand. I will be spared. My son will be spared. We will live peacefully in exile. As for you, your head can be cut open in front of all of Benoni for all I care! I have specifically added that to my demands," Maina said while grinning.

FREDRICK'S HANDS WERE tied in chains as he was dragged to the ground where the slave auction was about to take place. Two men, Diara and Doli were dragging the chains of the slaves. They would jerk them from time to time to make them move faster.

"How much for the white one?" a man wearing a hood asked Diara.

"More than you can pay, Laken," Diara laughed as he shrugged off Laken and kept moving.

"How about two horses?" Laken offered as he kept chasing Diara.

"How about you disappear from my sight?" Diara spat.

"Four horses and free visits to the brothel," Laken bargained.

Diara stopped walking and turned to look at Laken, who was busy eyeing Fredrick.

"How many visits?" Diara asked.

"As many as your heart desires," Laken responded.

Kofi, another slave of the clan who had developed a bond with Fredrick nudged him, gesturing for him to look at the exchange going on between Diara and Laken.

"He's selling you to him," Kofi said.

Fredrick had become too used to the slave trade. He had been getting sold from one enslaver to the other. He never served one for too long since someone else would spot him and put a price on him owing to the color of his skin.

"I will also take the one with him," Laken told Diara, gesturing at Kofi.

"I suppose we have to stick together now," Fredrick said.

"We won't be together. I'll be out there doing the filthiest chores and you won't be expected to get your hands dirty," Kofi said.

Fredrick sighed. He was aware of why he was valued above the other dark-skinned slaves. He was light-skinned and the slave owners believed that if he mated with their dark-skinned slaves, the children were likely to turn out light-skinned. This would allow the slave owners to sell them at a higher price once they grew up.

Fredrick was a popular choice for the people who bought him, mostly to use as a stud slave. He was handed over to slave traders for the purpose of producing children and his demand had been so high that he had been turned into a traveling stud slave.

"Get these two on the boat," Laken instructed his men.

Fredrick and Kofi were taken to the boat, where other slaves were also huddled up on the deck. They were told to stand in a queue so they could be counted. Fredrick also followed the instructions and lined up among the rest of the slaves.

"Where are you looking?" Kofi asked Fredrick as he spotted him staring at the deck of the boat.

"Our escape," Fredrick told him.

The slaves weren't given a proper place to sleep, so they had to lie down on the deck to sleep. When everyone had fallen asleep, Fredrick woke up Kofi and gestured for him to follow him.

"I'm chained," Kofi told Fredrick.

Fredrick took out a dagger that was hidden in his clothes. He picked the lock on the chains that were on Kofi's wrists and once they had managed to get rid of the chains, Fredrick ran to the dinghy, trying to find a way to throw it into the water beside the shore.

"It's heavy," Kofi told Fredrick.

Both Fredrick and Kofi somehow managed to throw the dinghy into the water. The sound woke up the guards that were supposed to keep an eye on the slaves. They ran to stop Fredrick and Kofi, who made a mad dash and tried to jump into the water before they could catch them.

Unfortunately, one of the guards managed to catch Kofi's leg and pulled him back. He looked at Fredrick, who was struggling in the water, trying to get control of the dinghy.

"Stop right there, or he gets killed!" the guard threatened as he held a knife to Kofi's throat.

Kofi had been Fredrick's only confidant and support ever since he was sold to the slave traders. They had been traveling together, and he just couldn't abandon him. Fredrick decided to return to the boat for Kofi's sake.

"You're lucky that your skin color is different than the rest, or you would have gotten a whipping you wouldn't be able to forget for the rest of your life," Laken told Fredrick as he grabbed him by his neck.

However, he was still angry at his attempt to run away and wanted to punish him. Laken took out an axe, and without any warning, he lobbed off one of Fredrick's toes, causing the blood to spurt across the deck. Fredrick moaned, trying to suppress his screams as the agony crippled him.

"If you try to escape again, you'll lose another toe," Laken warned him. Then he spat at Fredrick's face as he walked away from him, leaving him bleeding profusely.

Chapter 28: A New Heritage

PEDRO HAD BEEN OCCUPIED with planning a strategy for Ookpala. He was aware that Ookpala was furious at Maina, and he was also looking to find his children. He had to find a way to help Ookpala by providing justice to the lives that Maina had ruined, but he also wanted him to be cautious. This captive that he had to recover was no other than his own son!

It was the first council meeting since Omonoma's arrest. Pedro sat on the council along with Ookpala and Iredia as they discussed the fate of the prisoners.

"You are all aware of the malice spread by Maina and his conspiracies that have brought us to this stage. I have wanted to execute him publicly but as much as I dislike him, he is the key to finding my sons and my grandson. We are now considering a royal pardon in exchange for information about my family," Ookpala informed the council.

"I think we shouldn't rush with the royal pardon," Pedro offered his opinion.

"What do you suggest?" Ookpala asked.

"We're still missing Fredrick. If Maina has sold Fredrick into slavery, then I don't think he has gotten too far by now. We should be able to follow his trail," Pedro insisted.

"How are we supposed to find him?" Chief Odunsi asked.

"I have been part of a crew that has been liberating slaves for decades. I know my way around. I'm certain we can find Fredrick. I just need some time," Pedro proposed.

"Fredrick came here to rescue me. He knew the risks but he still chose this. He deserves Benoni's efforts to recover him," Ookpala weighed in.

"I agree," Iredia said.

"After we have recovered Fredrick, we can consider Maina's plea for banishment in exchange for his assistance to help us find Peter," Pedro said.

The council decided to accept Pedro's suggestion, but Pedro wasn't finished yet. He had something more to say.

"I would also like to propose something very important to me and my mother," Pedro glanced at Iredia.

Iredia knew what he was going to say. He had expressed his wish to her before, but she didn't have the heart to bring it up in front of the council.

"Captain Joaquim was the father I had known all my life. He gave me an abundance of love and protected me from the world. I would like to lay him to rest with a proper funeral," Pedro said.

"I would also like to have a funeral for Efe. I know he passed away a while ago, but his death was kept hidden from me. He was loyal to me till his last breath. Efe deserves a royal funeral for his service to me," Ookpala said.

"Very well. The Red Palace will have a funeral for both Captain Joaquim and Efe," Chief Odunsi weighed in.

"I will depart with the crew of the African Queen as soon as we are finished with the funerals," Pedro said.

"I will also come with you, Ookpala stated. Omo will be in charge of affairs in my absence."

"And me," Iredia added.

Pedro looked at both of them with gratitude and then nodded.

OBA OOKPALA'S PALACE pastor, Kendis, officiated the funeral. Benoni gathered around the Red Palace to pay respect to the deceased Captain Joaquim and Efe. The funeral didn't include the bodies of the two people since they had already been buried.

"We are gathered here to honor the lives of Captain Joaquim and Efe. Although Captain Joaquim didn't belong to Benoni, he risked his life to rescue Oba Ookpala. Sadly, he is not here with us anymore, but his courage will be remembered by the generations to come," Pastor Kendis addressed the crowd gathered for the funeral.

Queen Iredia laid her head tie on the pyre made for Captain Joaquim. She whispered to him with tears in her eyes.

"Thank you, Joaquim, for caring for me and my son. I wish you a peaceful rest and reunion with Lushinna, your beloved wife."

Pedro held onto his mother's hand. Tears streamed down his face silently as his last tribute to his adopted father.

Pedro let go of his mother's hand and told her to go to Ookpala. Iredia found her way through the crowd to reach Ookpala, who was standing in the corner and witnessing the funeral of his beloved servant and friend, Efe.

She held Ookpala's hand while looking at him. Ookpala grabbed Iredia and guided her away from the crowd along with him. Ookpala turned to her and sighed.

"Maina had many confessions to make about Omonoma and Omo," Ookpala told Iredia.

"Tell me."

"Omonoma is not my son," Ookpala revealed.

"How is it possible? Didn't the priestess give birth to him?" Iredia asked, confused.

"She gave birth to someone else. It was Omo. Maina exchanged Omo with his son, Omonoma, so he could rule through him," Ookpala told Iredia. "I don't trust Maina, but that doesn't change the fact that I have always loved Omo like I would have loved my children. I wish to acknowledge him as my son. However, I struggle because of the circumstances of his conception. I do not wish to acknowledge a son of the god Otun as mine. He is an abominable seed."

Iredia was lost for words. She had doubts about the paternity of Omonoma but didn't expect that Omo was his son. Iredia was still struggling with Ookpala's infidelity, and it was another blow to her pride. However, she was born again and had been so since Yola.

"Is Omo a born-again believer in Jesus Christ? " Iredia asked Ookpala.

"Yes, he is. I led him to Christ myself when I was imprisoned. He accepted Jesus as his lord and savior years ago," Ookpala answered.

"Then that is all that matters. The circumstances of his physical conception pale in comparison to his rebirth in Christ. As a born-again Christian, the tie to god Otun is nullified. He is not a child of the god Otun but a child of the one true God.

"Since the one true God sent his only son Jesus to die in his place and has called him his son, who is Otun or you to call him different or abominable?" Iredia asked him.

"The day Omonoba accepted Jesus as his lord and savior, he became a new creature. His heritage is now in Christ and no longer in god Otun. So, my dear husband, you know what to do. Let us go back to the funeral."

Ookpala heaved a huge sigh of relief as he realized that what Iredia had just said was the truth. The truth of God's word was the only truth that mattered.

It was evident to Ookpala that Iredia didn't want to discuss the matter any further. He was, however, happy that God had given him such a wise wife. He, however, also respected her reservations as a woman and a mother.

OOKPALA ANNOUNCED THAT he was going to address the council after the funeral. No one left the Red Palace after the funeral and the chiefs gathered around to hear what Ookpala had to say. Omo was told to sit next to Ookpala during the council meeting.

It was the first time Omo had been a part of the meeting which left him feeling confused. He didn't understand why Ookpala had made it clear that he wanted Omo to sit next to him.

"We all had a long day today. We gave a last farewell to our loved ones and put their souls to rest. Now that they have departed from this world and we have honored them with a funeral, I would like to make an announcement that will be crucial for the future of Benoni," Ookpala began. "I was fed lies about my son from the coronation ceremony for decades. I was told that the priestess gave birth to Omonoma and that I should declare him my heir. The truth is Omonoma was never my son. He was someone else's."

The council members were shocked and surprised by the news. But, Ookpala had more to reveal.

"Omo is the child who was given birth to by the priestess. His full name is Omonoba. Regardless of the circumstances of his birth, he has chosen to be re-born in Christ. Hence, I also want to acknowledge him as one of my sons today. From here on out, he shall be known as Prince Omonoba. He will be entitled to all the benefits of being a prince of this kingdom," Ookpala announced. "However, the lineage for throne inheritance will remain strictly with the children I sired from my marriage to Queen Iredia."

The entire council went silent as they listened to Ookpala. Omo was merely a servant of the Red Palace. They didn't expect him to be the son of the Oba.

Omo sat there next to Ookpala, unable to express himself. He fell short of words. He had been serving Ookpala for years and always regarded him as the father he never had. He looked at Ookpala with astonishment on his face; Ookpala's nodded at Omo, encouraging him to accept the truth.

After the council calmed down after hearing this, Ookpala revealed another surprising piece of news for them.

"I will be traveling with the African Queen, along with Queen Iredia. We must find my sons and my grandson, all of whom have been sold into slavery. I hope you will await my arrival as I will return soon with good news for all of Benoni."

Chapter 29: Destiny

PEDRO HAD BEEN LEADING the crew of the African Queen on the quest to find Fredrick for five months now. Pedro knew his way around the sea and had the advantage of having a strong network among the captains of the seafaring community.

However, it was still frustrating for him. He would hear about Fredrick's whereabouts from his informants and follow the lead, but by the time he'd reach the place, Fredrick would already have departed from the location.

It was the fourth time he had been informed about Fredrick's location. He knew that chances for him and the crew to finally retrieve Fredrick were low, but he insisted on continuing the search. After all, Fredrick was his only son and he couldn't give up on the hope of finding him.

The African Queen docked at a remote island. Pedro had been informed that his son was shipped there as a slave.

"I will come along," Ookpala told Pedro as he prepared to leave for the island.

As Pedro and Ookpala stepped on the island and walked toward the hut where Pedro's informant lived, they saw a man running in their direction.

"You're the captain of the African Queen, right?" the man asked Pedro.

"Yes, I'm looking for-"

Pedro was interrupted before he could tell him about his informant.

"Diara left the island last night. I'm Doli. He told me to tell you that Fredrick departed from the island last week with his new slave owner," Doli told Pedro.

Pedro didn't even wait for Doli to say anything else. He returned to the boat with Ookpala following him behind. Ookpala had gotten old and couldn't keep up with his son. When they reached the boat, Ookpala started panting.

"Pedro," Ookpala called, making him turn.

"Why did you two return so early?" Iredia asked as she saw her husband and son back on the boat.

Pedro bowed his head down, making Iredia realize that, once again, he couldn't find his son. Fredrick was still out there somewhere but they couldn't catch up to him.

"I think we should consider Maina's proposition to let him help us find Fredrick," Iredia told Ookpala.

"We will have to offer him exemption from execution in exchange for his help. He wants exile and me to execute Mishkia," Ookpala responded.

Iredia turned her back and marched toward her chamber. She felt hopeless. They had been trying to find Fredrick but just couldn't. He was slipping out from their hands like sand.

"Come with me," Ookpala told Pedro.

When Ookpala and Pedro reached Iredia's chamber, they found her shattered. She was crying, tired and devastated.

"I kept trying to find you for decades. I did everything I could to find your trace but couldn't. I was convinced that I had failed. I felt defeated and weak. But something happened that altered our destiny," Ookpala told her. "I bowed in front of the one true God, Jesus Christ. I repented and asked for his help. It was only then that you somehow found your way back to me. We don't need any traitor's help, Iredia. We need Jesus. His grace will be sufficient for us."

Iredia sobbed as she listened to Ookpala. She looked up at him with tears in her eyes.

"Indeed. God said the man is the head of the family. Whatever the head says, or does, affects his whole family. That is why the family's name comes from the head of the household.

"Will God still help us? Will God help us find our grandson? All I have done most of my life is worship Him. First, my twins were taken from me. Now my only grandson is a slave somewhere," Iredia sobbed.

"He will, he will. I am sure he will. Let us pray the prayer of agreement together," Ookpala answered.

Ookpala, Iredia, and Pedro joined hands and went on their knees. They called for divine intervention. They prayed for the restoration of their families. They decreed on Earth and agreed that it was decreed in Heaven, that their family would be restored without the aid of a traitor.

After that day, Iredia made up her mind and devoted her time to praying to God along with Ookpala. They spent their nights kneeling in front of God, asking Him for mercy and help.

AFTER AN ENTIRE MONTH of keeping Fredrick as a stud slave on his boat, Laken decided to sell him to a wealthy slave owner. He had been offered a great price for Fredrick and saw it as the perfect opportunity to make money.

"Hurry up, Jackerville is right there," Laken told Fredrick as he gestured in the direction in front of him.

Fredrick, Laken, and his men arrived at the plantation. It was one of the biggest plantations that Fredrick had ever seen. As soon as they arrived at the main house, Fredrick saw a tall man walking in their direction. Laken extended his arms to embrace the tall man.

"It's been a long time, Borsan," Laken said as they embraced.

"You have grown old," Borsan said as he patted Laken's shoulder.

"Look what I have brought for you," Laken stated as he gestured at Fredrick.

"I will keep him here for a week for his stud services. You can take him back after that," Borsan told Laken.

"You said you wanted to buy him," Laken whispered in Borsan's ears.

"I will. I need to see if he's worth it," Borsan responded roughly.

Fredrick was supposed to stay at the plantation for the week. It was decided that he would be given a place to sleep during his stay. He shared his quarters with another slave, Manasee, who was the foreman of the Jackerville's plantation and had been living there for decades.

The second night of Fredrick's stay, the stables in the plantation caught fire and every slave was woken up. They were told to help put out the fire.

"Grab those buckets," Manasee told Fredrick.

Fredrick picked up the buckets of water and ran toward the stable. He was standing in front of the stables when he heard a woman's screams. Fredrick didn't have time to think and he decided to go inside the stables to rescue the woman.

"Help!" the woman's voice echoed.

Fredrick managed to get rid of the planks in the way of him and the woman. Finally, he spotted the stuck woman. She was probably the same age as his father. He extended his hand so she could hold it and follow him out of the stables.

Soon, Fredrick and the woman made it out of the stables. When they had safely reached outside, Fredrick turned to the woman, and to his surprise, she was staring at him with an astonished face.

"Your eyes...," she said.

"How did you end up in the stables?" Fredrick asked.

"I'm Borsan's wife, Marilla, but you..."

"My mother's name was also Marilla. She was white with blond hair as curly as yours." Fredrick told her.

"Who is your father?" Marilla asked as her heart started to beat faster.

"You wouldn't know him. He is the captain of the boat called the African Queen, Pedro-"

Marilla fell on her knees. She started sobbing while holding Fredrick's hand.

"Are you fine? What happened?" Fredrick asked, puzzled.

"Your name is Fredrick?"

"How do you know?"

It was then that Marilla told Fredrick that she was his mother. Fredrick couldn't believe his eyes; his mother was kneeling in front of him.

"Help!" Fredrick heard Borsan's voice.

Fredrick ran towards a burning shed. He saw that Borsan was stuck under a beam that had fallen on him. He tried to lift the beam but it was too heavy.

Marilla helped him lift it and together, they managed to rescue Borsan but it was too late. Borsan had suffered burns to a great extent. They rushed him to the main house but Borsan only managed to breathe for a few hours.

"He's gone," Fredrick told Marilla as she watched him and Manasee try to save Borsan.

Borsan's corpse was escorted by Manasee, who lifted him with the help of other slaves and they took him out. Marilla sat in the same spot, trying to contemplate the irony of the situation.

Borsan had bought her as a slave, but she ended up becoming his wife. He had grown fond of Marilla during his last years, but she couldn't let go of the fact that he had bought her.

"I'm sorry for your loss," Fredrick told Marilla.

Marilla caressed Fredrick's face as she looked at him with helpless eyes.

"At last, you're here," Marilla said. "Your father must have forgotten about me."

"He never did. If he did, he would have re-married. He thought you abandoned him. But he never stopped loving you." Fredrick explained.

"Marilla's face brightened on hearing that Pedro still loved her."

Fredrick sat down with Marilla and narrated his story about how he ended up in Benoni, which led him to be sold into slavery. He was speaking about Benoni when he saw Manasee standing behind him.

"Did you say you were in Benoni?" Manasee asked.

"Yes. How do you know about the place?"

"I was kidnapped from Benoni when I was a child. I'm the son of Benoni's Oba. I do not remember the details, all I know is one day, I was a prince, and the next I was a slave. I woke up, and found myself tied in chains on a boat. I have not seen my parents since that day. My first owner changed my name from Peter to Manasee-"

"Peter? Are you one of Oba Ookpala's twins?" Fredrick asked incredulously.

"Yes! I have an identical twin brother. His name is Paul but I don't know about the whereabouts of my twin. We were separated," Manasee explained.

"Ookpala is my grandfather and Iredia is my grandmother," Fredrick confessed.

"How? My brother...Paul?" Manasee stammered, confused.

Fredrick told him about his father, Pedro, who was Manasee's brother and Ookpala and Iredia's third son. Manasee looked at Fredrick with disbelief. He was trembling as he realized the truth. Destiny had brought Ookpala's son and grandson together.

Fredrick spent the entire night explaining the events that happened in Benoni, leading to him discovering that his grandmother Cleo, was actually Queen Iredia, the lost Queen of the Benoni Kingdom.

Chapter 30: Freedom

"PRINCE OMO, PLEASE get up!"

Omo woke up when he heard Kojo's familiar voice. He was one of Ookpala's advisors who was the same age as Omo.

"What is it?" Omo asked, annoyed by the interruption in his sleep.

"The African Queen is docking," Kojo informed him.

Suddenly, Omo hopped up from his bed. He was wide awake now that he had heard the name of the African Queen.

"They must have found Fredrick!" Omo said as he dressed.

The shadow of the huge African Queen was cast on the coast of Benoni. The Red Palace's servants, chiefs, and advisors gathered around to welcome their Oba, who was onboard the African Queen and returning home after more than a year.

Jimmy was the first person to climb down the stairs to the dock, followed by Queen Iredia and Oba Ookpala. Omo made his way through the crowd that had gathered around them. Finally, he saw Ookpala but was surprised that he didn't appear to be in high spirits.

"Did you find him?" Omo asked.

Ookpala didn't have the courage to answer him, but Omo understood that their quest to find Fredrick hadn't been successful. He met with the crowd and his chiefs before leaving for the Red Palace. A few hours after arriving at Benoni, Ookpala asked Kojo to send Omo to his chamber.

"Father, you asked for me?" Omo asked.

"Yes, I did. I want to talk to you about something," Ookpala said as he sat down in a chair near his bed.

Omo nodded.

"We spent fifteen months in the sea, searching for Fredrick. Sometimes we came close but not close enough. He was getting moved around and finally, we lost his trace. I didn't want to bow down to Maina and his schemes but Pedro's spirit has been broken," Ookpala confessed.

"Where is Pedro now?" Omo asked.

"He is still out there trying to find his son. I want this madness to come to an end. We will have to come to terms with Maina's bargain in exchange for his help to find my family," Ookpala explained.

It wasn't the kind of news that anyone was expecting. It was not going to lift the spirits of Benoni. Ookpala was considering a royal pardon for his foe who had schemed to ruin his life but Omo could understand Ookpala's sentiments. After all, Pedro was his son and he had to do everything possible to unite him with his only child.

"Maina will be thrilled to hear about the new development," Omo said bitterly.

"It's my last resort, Omo. Please see to the necessary matters for the royal pardon," Ookpala said as he returned to his bed.

Omo walked back to his chamber and asked Kojo to join him for a discussion with the chiefs present in the Red Palace. It was decided that Omo would inform Maina of the preparations for his royal pardon. He would have to sit through the explanation of the royal pardon's decorum.

"Open the gates," Omo told the dungeon guards where Maina was imprisoned.

As Omo walked up to Maina, he saw him grinning. That caught him by surprise. It seemed as if Maina was already aware of the situation in the Red Palace. He seemed very pleased with himself.

"We require your presence in the Great Hall this evening, where you will have a discussion about your royal pardon," Omo told Maina.

"At last, your Oba has come to his senses! I told him he wouldn't find Fredrick without my help but he didn't listen to me. He has wasted his valuable time," Maina laughed and gloated.

Omo didn't wish to engage any further with Maina and left the dungeon immediately after delivering the news of his royal pardon.

MAINA WAS ESCORTED to the Great Hall in the evening. He was brought out in chains and told to sit down and await the arrival of Ookpala's advisors. Kojo arrived shortly after with a parchment. He stared at Maina with disdain before speaking.

"I'm here to lay out the conditions for your royal pardon. You will be granted royal pardon once the Oba allows you to kiss his scepter-"

Kojo was interrupted by Maina's laughter.

"You might want to listen to my demands first. After all, I'm going to reunite your Oba with his family," Maina said viciously. "I want my demands to be written down in that very parchment so your Oba can't get away with them once I have been banished."

"Let us know your demands then," Kojo retorted curtly.

"First, I will be given the total sum of my estate to live out my life outside of Benoni in exile. Second, I will be accompanied by Omonoma. If he is not banished alongside me, I won't help your Oba," Maina said.

"Anything else?" Kojo stated.

"I want Mishkia's head."

After Maina was done with presenting his demands in exchange for his help, he was taken back to the dungeon. Ookpala was informed about Maina's demands by Omo. He was furious at Maina's audacity.

"I will decide on what we have to do with him. We have to wait for Pedro's arrival so we can go ahead with the ceremony for the royal pardon. He is supposed to be here soon after gathering information about Fredrick's whereabouts," Ookpala told Omo.

BORSAN WAS LAID TO rest the following day after the fire. Marilla was his only living family and had to perform the last rites of her late husband and captor.

"Someone is here to see you," Manasee, who tended to the plantation, told Marilla.

Marilla had been widowed recently and no one had come to visit her. She assumed that no one outside the plantation was aware of her existence but she was wrong. When Marilla entered the sitting room, she saw an old man seated comfortably. He was talking to himself, but Marilla had to interrupt him.

"I'm Marilla. I was told you are here to see me."

The old man stood up and bowed to Marilla as she walked inside the room.

"My apologies. I'm Jamar, Borsan's estate planner. You might not have heard of me since Borsan liked to keep people who dealt with his estate away from the plantation," Jamar smiled as he introduced himself.

"No, I had no idea you had business with my late husband," Marilla said.

"Now you do. I'm here to inform you about the future of Borsan's estate. Borsan never sired any heirs who could inherit his estate. His past wives mysteriously died, and you're the only remaining family he has, which leaves you with the entirety of the estate that he owned," Jamar told Marilla.

Marilla was left in a state of astonishment. She had served a man who had imprisoned her for a huge part of her life. She never expected to get anything out of him.

"I'm well aware of the kind of person Borsan was. I'm certain that he didn't wed you for love. Now is the time for you to get what is yours by right. You're the new owner of the Jackerville plantation," Jamar said while bringing out some papers that needed Marilla's signatures.

She signed the deed transfer papers with Jamar promising to file them accordingly.

"Thank you for taking the time to come all the way to tell me about this," Marilla said.

"It is my job. There are tax implications from your inheritance. When you have the time, prior to sixty days, come down to the railway mail service office in town to pay the estate taxes. You will need me to do so. My office is right across the hall from theirs."

"I will. Once again, thank you."

After that, Jamar left, leaving behind two huge sacks of money. Overjoyed, Marilla asked for both Fredrick and Manasee to come and see her immediately.

FREDRICK WAS IN HIS quarters when suddenly, Laken showed up. He had returned after hearing about Borsan's demise. He had instructed Fredrick to pack up, as he already had another client lined up for him who needed his stud services. Fredrick told him about the fire and the delay in providing the service, but Laken wasn't interested.

"Time is money," he stated. "Borsan paid for one week's worth of time, so serviced or not, tomorrow morning, we are leaving Jackerville Plantation."

"YOU ASKED FOR ME?" Manasee said as soon as he entered the sitting room.

"Where is Fredrick?" Marilla asked when she saw that Fredrick hadn't come.

"Laken is here," Manasee informed her.

Marilla got up from her chair, picked up a sack, and walked to the farm to find Fredrick. She found him in the midst of an argument with Larken. Marilla walked right up to Laken, drawing his attention.

"Count," Marilla ordered as she gave the sack to Laken, who appeared clueless.

"What is it?" Laken asked.

"The price for Fredrick's freedom," Marilla told Laken.

Laken opened the sack and shuffled through the gold coins and some hometown notes. He was wide-eyed and couldn't believe what was happening. A greedy grin appeared on his face after he was done inspecting the contents of the sack.

"Who knew you could trade?" Laken grinned. "He's yours."

Laken left the plantation with the sack containing his newly earned wealth. Fredrick turned to Marilla, looking at her with astonishment in his eyes.

"How did you get that sack?" Fredrick asked.

"There is more. Jackerville belongs to me now and I have decided that we will rent a boat and a crew to travel to Benoni."

"Benoni?" Fredrick asked eagerly.

"Yes. We can't keep waiting for the African Queen to rescue us. Pedro is clueless about our whereabouts. We will have to make the journey ourselves," Marilla told Fredrick.

Since Manasee had spent the majority of his life in the Jackerville Plantation, he knew where he could find a boat for their journey. He managed to gather a crew of sailors and a boat that would take them to Benoni.

Marilla liberated all the slaves working on the plantation before leaving for the journey. She then turned around and offered jobs to those who were willing to stay at the plantation in exchange for food, board, and a stipend. Some of the slaves accepted the job offers. Some chose to leave.

Together, Marilla, Fredrick, and Manasee set sail for the destination that awaited them.

Chapter 31: Royal Pardon

"IT'S TIME," PEDRO'S voice echoed in Ookpala's chamber.

Ookpala had been walking in circles the entire night. He couldn't get any sleep owing to the anticipation of the next day. The pardoning ceremony was supposed to start in the afternoon, and Ookpala hadn't spoken to anyone since the morning.

Ookpala turned around to see Pedro standing at the door along with his mother, Iredia. Her head was bowed and she tried not to look into Ookpala's eyes. She knew all too well that Maina had humiliated Ookpala in front of Benoni but she and her husband didn't have any choice left.

Maina was the last resort for finding Ookpala's twin sons and Fredrick and he was hellbent on taking advantage of the situation to strike a bargain for his freedom and kill Mishkia, his disloyal wife.

THE PARDONING CEREMONY was about to start in the Great Hall. Omo walked up to the dungeon and instructed the guards to escort Maina out.

Ookpala arrived to find everyone gathered in front of his throne. The Great Hall was filled with servants and guards of the Red Palace and the Old Palace. All the chiefs who were part of the council were also present, along with the Oba's family.

Ookpala sat down on his throne as Maina kneeled in front of him beneath the stairs of the throne's platform. Maina's head was bowed, but his grin was still visible from across the Great Hall. He was no longer in chains which made for an unpleasant sight for Ookpala.

An older man with a long beard, wearing a long ivory robe, stood next to Ookpala's throne.

"I, Pastor Kendis of the Red Palace, bless this ceremony for pardoning Chief Maina for the traitorous sins he has committed against the Crown and the Kingdom of Benoni," he announced.

"Oba Ookpala has granted me his permission to officiate this ceremony. I would now like to request the royal scepter of Pardon."

Pastor Kendis gestured at Prince Omo.

Omo began to walk toward the holding room for the scepter but saw a young man whispering to Kojo, leaving him uncertain, as Kojo beckoned to him. He saw Kojo staring at the young man, wide-eyed. Kojo turned around to face Omo, who was about to reach out for the scepter.

"Omo, something has happened," Kojo whispered to him.

"What is it?" Omo asked.

"A boat has docked at Benoni's shore. They're saying that it's Fredrick," Kojo said.

"What?"

Omo left the scepter, and rushed toward the throne, making his way swiftly to Ookpala. He whispered in Ookpala's ears as Maina stared at them suspiciously.

"Is this real? Is he here?" Ookpala asked, astonished. Omo nodded.

Maina was struck by the realization that something was happening around him. He stood up quickly and reached for Ookpala's arm.

"Finish this ceremony," Maina commanded with blood in his eyes.

Before Ookpala could respond, Kojo unsheathed his machete and severed Maina's extended hand, causing blood to splash all over the throne.

"Seize him!" Omo commanded.

Immediately, the guards seized Maina and put him in chains while he howled in pain, holding on to the stump of his wrist.

"Take me to him," Ookpala said to Omo.

"My Oba, please wait. Let us get to the bottom of this matter," Kojo told Ookpala, who had gotten up from his throne.

"It's my grandson. I have to confirm it for myself," Ookpala said before leaving his throne.

Ookpala marched towards the gate of the Great Hall as people whispered and stared at him. The chiefs tried to stop him but he refused to listen.

"Are you certain?" Pedro asked Omo. He heard Fredrick's name and just like Ookpala, he was restless and wanted to know if it was true.

"I believe so. People have witnessed it," Omo said.

Pedro also left the Great Hall, following Ookpala. Iredia watched as her husband and son left the ceremony. She was still clueless about the new development but she decided to follow after Ookpala's trail and see what all the fuss was about.

"Where are you going and what about the pardoning ceremony?" Iredia asked when she caught up with Ookpala and Pedro, who marched through the gates of the Red Palace.

"Trust me, Iredia. You and I will both find out," Ookpala replied firmly.

When Ookpala, Pedro, and Iredia reached outside, they saw Fredrick walking toward them. Pedro couldn't believe his eyes when he saw his son. He ran to hug him, laughing with tears of joy shining in his eyes.

"My boy! My boy!" he exclaimed with happiness.

Then he saw a woman walking behind Fredrick. Pedro stopped abruptly. He couldn't believe what he was seeing.

It was Marilla, his long-lost wife.

Fredrick was still embracing Pedro, who remained astonished as he saw Marilla. Fredrick started weeping, but Pedro's eyes were fixated on his lost wife.

"Pedro," she said.

Hearing Marilla's voice sent shivers down Pedro's spine. Yet, he looked at her in disbelief.

"It's her. I found her," Fredrick reassured Pedro.

"I thought you left me forever," Pedro finally said.

Marilla took Pedro's hand and kissed it.

"I never did. I was kidnapped. At last, I have found you," Marilla said with tears in her eyes.

As Ookpala and Iredia went to embrace Fredrick, he saw that he was accompanied by a man whose eyes seemed strangely familiar, and before Ookpala could say anything, he had extended his hand. Ookpala shook his hand and spotted the tribal markings on the side of his left eye!

"Peter?" Iredia whispered in shock, standing beside Ookpala.

Ookpala looked at Fredrick and he nodded.

"They changed my name to Manasee when I was first sold," Peter told Ookpala.

Both Ookpala and Iredia embraced Peter. Iredia broke down, sobbing as she held her son.

"How did you find him, Fredrick?" Ookpala asked his grandson.

"I will tell you everything," Fredrick reassured Ookpala.

"What about Paul?" Ookpala asked, looking around.

Fredrick's silence served as the answer to Ookpala's question. It marred his happiness to know that while he had finally united with his family, he was still clueless about Paul's whereabouts.

Despite that, it was a happy reunion.

Oba Ookpala declared festivities in Benoni kingdom for ten days.

OMO HAD MANAGED TO retrieve information about the entire ring of slave traders who had been arrested and were being detained in the dungeon since Chief Maina was initially captured. They were waiting for their sentence.

A week after Oba Ookpala was united with his family and all the festivities were rounded up. All the prisoners were summoned to be presented in the Great Hall. Oba Ookpala was supposed to declare sentences for all those who had betrayed the throne.

Ookpala sat on his throne as he geared up to declare the sentences of the prisoners.

"All of you are here because you have betrayed the throne. Maina and Esoha will be executed immediately for their treason against the throne and their attempt to eradicate my family!" Ookpala declared as he stared at Maina. "Slave traders will remain imprisoned for the rest of their lives and will do hard labor while they serve their sentence!"

Then he turned to address Mishkia.

"As for Mishkia, you could have saved my family but you didn't. You are also a traitor to the throne. I'm sparing you from execution since you played an important role in bringing my family back together. You will be banished from Benoni and you're never to set foot inside this land for the rest of your life," Ookpala declared.

Mishkia kept her eyes lowered and accepted her fate.

"As for you Omonoma, you are a victim of circumstances as well. Indeed you are not my son nor god Otun's son. I would imprison you for not executing me when you had me in chains. However, there is only one sentence that suits treason. You will be executed alongside your biological father."

After Ookpala declared the sentences, he summoned the chiefs of the council. They all gathered around as Ookpala addressed them.

"Benoni will rise again. We have to build Benoni all over again, and it will start with the rightful succession. Peter will succeed me as the Oba. He is my first-born, followed by Paul, should he ever be recovered, then Pedro, my third son.

The first-born son of any sitting Oba will have a superior claim to the throne before any brothers to a deceased Oba," he announced.

"Omo is also a son from my loins. Albeit, he is not from my marriage to Queen Iredia. He and his lineage will always have a place in the palace. They will be second only to the sitting Oba. This second-in-command position will be inherited as well. It will be carried on through his lineage. The title for the second-in-command position shall henceforth be Eyasera of Benoni Kingdom."

Then, he looked at his council firmly.

"I don't wish to hear anyone contest the appointment of Omo. He is also my son and he has fought for me when no one else did," Ookpala told the council. There was no contest. The chiefs were happy that Oba Ookpala had finally accepted the son of the bloody coronation.

At last, there was peace in Benoni and Ookpala's family.

Epilogue: Restoration

OOKPALA WAS LYING IN his bed with two young children beside him; they had become drowsy. Ookpala's hair and beard had turned gray, and he could barely sit. He was supported by a pillow behind his back as he narrated his story to his grandchildren.

"He who breaks the edge, the serpent will bite! God says thou shall not serve any other gods except for me, but you see, at my coronation event, I served idols and committed adultery to ascend the throne.

"Thereafter, the serpent bit. I suffered! I had four children but I suffered their loss and spent most of my life without their presence. My fate wouldn't have been turned if I hadn't knelt in front of God and asked for His forgiveness.

"When I repented of my sin and gave myself up to God, He blessed me by giving me back my lost family, returning them to me from the furthest places on Earth," Ookpala said.

"So you suffered because you went against God's word?" Odi, Peter's daughter, asked.

"Yes. God's word is supreme, and it must be obeyed. The Lord used me and my brother Oba Osu to change the traditions of Benoni that held back its people. Today, the wives of the Obas are not buried with the Obas. Worship of the god Otun is completely abolished in Benoni. The bloody coronation that required siring heirs for the reserve is abolished. Also, most importantly, twins are left alive at birth. We now celebrate them and covet them as blessings from God," Ookpala said with a chuckle. "We no longer have slaves in Benoni, we have palace servants. The heritage of traditionally approved human sacrifice and slavery is a lost heritage forever. It will never return to Benoni."

"The power of Christ used me and my family's situation to break the bondage of darkness in Benoni. Our new and only heritage is in Christ. In Christ, there is peace, joy, love, and family," he continued. "As you grow older, you must tell everyone to accept Jesus Christ as the savior of their life. They have to believe in their hearts and confess with their mouths that Jesus is the son of the one true God, he died and was resurrected. People must accept him as the lord of their lives and they will be saved."

Seeing that the twins were half asleep, he smiled.

"It's also time for you two to sleep," Ookpala said warmly.

"You didn't tell us what happened after you united with your family," Owoh, Peter's son, yawned.

"Well, I and Chaga's prayers from when I was in Yola for Peter were answered. Your father became the Crown Prince of Benoni. Later, I ceded my throne to him as I had grown old. Your father became Benoni's Oba.

"Marilla didn't want to return to the plantation where she was held against her will. Pedro and Marilla decided to return to Saba Island and the African Queen. They left Fredrick to run the Jackerville plantation," Ookpala adjusted the pillow behind him.

"What about grandma?" Odi asked.

"Your grandmother and I have retired from the politics of the throne. We want to spend our remaining time with our grandchildren in peace. Our life journeys had been unexpected and eventful indeed, we knew we had a role to play in converting the people of Benoni to Christianity, but we did not know the method, the personal sacrifice, nor the length of time it would take." Ookpala continued.

"Odi and Owoh, it's time for bed," Iredia declared as she walked inside Ookpala's chamber.

"Here she is, my love," Ookpala smiled.

Odi and Owoh left the chamber as Iredia knelt beside Ookpala.

"Are you tired?" Iredia asked as she helped Ookpala get off his bed to his knees for their bedtime prayer.

"I was once a very tired man when I didn't have my family besides me. Now I can never get tired of this life. You have completed my life," Ookpala said.

After they finished their bedtime prayer, Ookpala closed his eyes as Iredia climbed into the bed beside him and lay down. She held his hand as they drifted off to sleep.

THE END

About the Author

Phyllis Asibor is a born-again child of God. An American nursing professional with African roots. She holds two degrees, one in insurance and the second in nursing. She is a certified registered nurse case manager. She has a love for fiction. She is a dreamer and prone to fantasies.

She represented the country of Nigeria twice at the World Chess Olympiads. She has history in Nigerian modeling and acting. Phyllis enjoys the word of God. She loves taking photos, acting, talking, writing, watching movies, traveling, and playing Scrabble. She enjoys helping others.

Phyllis desired to write a book that would deliver the message that a person planted in Christ changes their heritage. When they accept Christ, their roots are transformed. They sprout from the word of God. Their fruits become fruits of excellence.

She started writing as a hobby. She was inspired to write *"Lost Heritage: Royals in Slave Clothes"* from a revelation that, as children of God, all people are of royal heritage. Your human heritage is insignificant compared to your spiritual heritage in Christ.

"Lost Heritage: Royals in Slave Clothes" is Phyllis's first novel.

Thank you for reading her book.